DIVIDED

Jennifer Sights

Author Info:

Website: www.JenniferSights.com
Facebook: http://www.facebook.com/jennifersightswrites
Email: jsights@gmail.com
Twitter: http://twitter.com/JenniferSights

ACKNOWLEDGEMENTS

I want to thank everyone who helped make this book possible. Jeremiah Koczan and James Holder for beta reading, Ellen Moeller for editing, and everyone in the Asymmetrical Community for the advice and support throughout the editing and publishing process. I have to give a huge thanks to the folks who run National Novel Writing Month, without which this book probably wouldn't have been written. Thanks to my parents for supporting me in everything I do. And of course thanks to my wonderful husband John for being unendingly supportive and patient while I spent hours on end holed up in my office working on the manuscript and figuring out all the details for publishing it.

Thanks to Denise Wy for the gorgeous cover design.
www.denisewy.com

Thanks to Casey Carrington of Chalk & Soot for author photograph.
chalkandsoot.com/index.html

Cover photo by chaoss / shutterstock.com

CHAPTER ONE

"Ms. Ronen, I need you to help me find my daughter, and I've heard you're the best." Alexis Carmen pushed a photograph toward me across my office desk. A pretty young girl with strawberry hair that matched her mother's smiled out of the photo.

"Please, call me Elena." I wanted to put Ms. Carmen at ease. Her brow furrowed, dark circles shadowed her honey brown eyes, making her porcelain skin look ever paler. A strand of hair strayed from her neat ponytail, which she absently tucked behind her ear.

"Elena. Courtney ran away two weeks ago."

"Have you contacted the police?" I asked.

"Yes, but because she is of legal age, they won't do anything."

I reflected on the few years I had spent on the force, and could imagine how frustrated Ms. Carmen must be. Eighteen is such an arbitrary age to be considered an adult. Some eighteen-year-olds are completely incapable of taking care of themselves. Others - like me, when I was younger - are more mature than many in their thirties. "How old is your daughter?"

"Nineteen." Her voice cracked, but not a single tear fell from her shining eyes. "The police referred me to you, actually. They said very good things about your ability to solve a case. Do you work with them often?"

"No, but I used to be a police officer."

"Why did you quit?"

"I didn't like all the red tape. I'd rather get something done than fill out stacks of paperwork." I stood. "Would you like some coffee, Mrs. Carmen?"

"Ms. And yes, thank you. Black."

The lack of sugar or cream matched the fit body beneath her slightly rumpled yet expensive looking business suit. I poured two cups of black coffee and handed her one. "Is there no Mr. Carmen?" I asked.

"No. But why does that matter?" She narrowed her eyes.

"Anything that can provide insight as to why your daughter might have run away could help. I'm sorry if it's a painful topic."

"I understand. I was always very focused on my education, but made one mistake that almost cost me my MBA. Do you have any idea how hard it is to complete graduate school while raising an infant?"

"I can imagine. Do you resent that hardship your daughter caused you by her birth?" I sipped my coffee and studied her reaction.

"Of course not!" Ms. Carmen straightened her shoulders and shook her head from side to side.

I raised an eyebrow.

"I admit it wasn't easy, but I wouldn't give up my daughter. I love her."

"Do you have a good relationship with your daughter?"

"I did, for the most part. But then she started attending St. Louis Community College. That's when the fighting began."

"What do you mean, 'for the most part?' "

"I was very strict with Courtney, and she often resented me for that, but she used to confide in me."

"What did you fight over?" I made note of the name of the college.

"Her degree. I wanted her to do something that would pay

well, but she's always loved art. I know firsthand how important it is for a young woman to not have to rely on a man, and I don't want my daughter to struggle. I was an art major, and ended up working fast food when I graduated. After a year, I went back to school for a business degree so I could make something of myself. I tried to tell her what I endured, tried to convince her to do better for herself, but she insisted on enrolling in the art program. And then she made new friends."

"What kind of friends?" I expected her to mention alcohol or drugs.

"Freaks."

I sat back in my chair, inadvertently putting more distance between myself and her.

She quickly glanced at my metal filled ears and the tattoo peeking from the sleeve of my scarlet blouse. "Forgive me. I mean Goths. I - I'm not used to - " she stammered, looking down into her lap and biting her lower lip.

I sighed, having mostly gotten used to remarks about my style long ago. "Forget it. So you didn't like her friends."

"No, and she changed. She dyed her hair black, started wearing tons of dark makeup, dressed like a vampire."

"So you fought about that as well?" I guessed.

"Yes. She started skipping classes. Her artwork became darker, more sinister. Then she ran away."

"How do you know she ran away? Could she have been kidnapped?"

"No, her clothes were gone, as well as her art supplies." She finally took a sip of her coffee, holding the mug in both hands.

"Have you contacted the college?"

"I have. Thankfully, I made her sign a waiver to let them release her information to me since she's over eighteen. They said she hasn't shown up to any classes in several weeks. I'm worried she's getting into drugs or something worse."

"Something worse?"

"Yes, I overheard her mention something about a coven while she was on the phone with one of her new friends. I'm afraid she's getting into some kind of Satanic cult or something. I don't understand what she meant by that." She gripped the mug so tightly I feared she would break it.

"Did you hear her mention anything else that might help? Do you know any of her friends' names, where they live, or where she hung out?"

"She was very secretive once we began fighting. I know one girl was named Miriam. Courtney's car had broken down - I made her work to pay for her own car and insurance - so this Miriam picked her up every day. I have no idea where they went, though."

"Can you describe Miriam?"

"I only saw her from a distance in the car, so, other than Goth, not really. I'm sorry; I realize that's no help. She drove a Chevy Malibu that looked several years old. Black, of course." Ms. Carmen paused, eyes closed.

"What else?"

"I heard her talk about someone named Elizabeth. She seemed to idolize her."

I paused while writing this down. "Is there anything else?"

"I can't think of anything. As much as we've fought recently, I love my daughter. I want her back." Her face brightened just a tiny bit with hope. "I've heard that you've never given up or failed on a case. Can you find her?"

" 'Never' is a bit of an exaggeration, but I'm sure I can find your daughter, Ms. Carmen. Try to relax." I stood, walked around the desk, and then handed Ms. Carmen a business card. "If you think of anything else that might help, please call me, anytime. I'll call you as soon as I find anything out."

"I'll warn you, the picture might not be much help. She looks completely different now, especially with all the makeup she wears."

I nodded. "I can't guarantee she'll come back home. As you

discovered from the police, she is legally able to do what she wants, but I'll at least be able to tell you where she is so you'll know she's safe."

She nodded, grasped my hand tightly, and then left.

Ms. Carmen's comment about "freaks" almost made me refuse the case, but it was an easy one, and she had already written me a check twice the size a case like this usually cost. However, something nagged at my gut. Something told me this wouldn't be as easy as it sounded.

CHAPTER TWO

Pounding music vibrated through the bar stool on which I sat at The Chapel - an old church converted into an eighteen-an-up Goth club. The bar was separated from the dance floor by a wrought iron fence that could have belonged in a millionaire's yard rather than a club. Two distinct groups of people filled the club.

The first was obviously out to live life to the fullest; some dancing alone, sweating, moving in their own world, others dancing with a member of the opposite - or same - sex, groping and grinding. How many had come with their dance partner, and how many were just there for the thrill of the night?

The other group lounged on red velvet chairs and couches, drinking from goblets, perfectly posed, determined to give off just the exact vibe and image of beauty and aloof dignity.

I was a loner and didn't go out much, so doubted anyone there would know me.

The bartender handed me another cranberry juice with a splash of tonic. I didn't drink. For one thing, alcohol and Zoloft don't mix. My past was less than enviable, and weekly therapy sessions hadn't done much good yet. Secondly, I'd done enough drinking and drugs in my teenage years - and enough stupid things because of that drinking - to make Satan weep. That is, if I believed in Satan. Which I didn't.

"I didn't order this," I said, still sipping my first drink.

"Compliments of Vittorio. He said to get you another of whatever you were already drinking," she said, looking toward the balcony which had acted as the choir loft in its previous life of -

you guessed it - a church.

"Vittorio? Is that his real name?" I shouted to be heard over the music.

"Believe it or not, it is. Full blooded Italian. Vittorio Santini."

A tall man with long black hair watched me from the balcony. "Is that him?"

The bartender nodded. After thanking her, I headed toward the balcony to introduce myself, and hopefully find something more about Courtney, Miriam, or Elizabeth. I wished for a more recent photo of Courtney, and any of the other two girls. "Goth" as a description would not help me find them. At the local Starbuck's, maybe, but not here. I had to start somewhere though, and I had learned to look at facial structures rather than makeup over the years.

The Chapel's website clearly stated the balcony was off limits to general club-goers. Some sort of VIP thing, I supposed, and the bouncer at the base of the stairs showed they were serious.

"Vittorio sent me a drink and I -"

He cut me off with a wave of his arm, indicating for me to go upstairs. Easier than I'd expected.

At the top of the stairs, confidence firmly in place, I saw the black hair was his natural color. It had highlights you just can't get out of a bottle. Sitting on a red velvet couch, he was the center of attention. He faced away from me, so I surveyed the area.

The crowd in the balcony belonged to the second group of club-goers, looking like extras straight out of a vampire movie. They weren't vampires, obviously - no such thing existed - but they'd sure pass. Some even had fake fangs.

The area was the size of a large living room. In back and to the right was a door with a sign that read "Restroom" and the image signifying it was for men and women. To the left was an unmarked door. A broom closet, maybe?

Vittorio turned and smiled at me. He was masculine in every way, yet his face managed to be beautiful. He was a god come to life; the most gorgeous, perfect creature to ever walk the face of the planet. Even that didn't do his beauty justice. This god actually smiled at me!

I shook my head. This groupie behavior would do no good. Taking a deep breath, I walked over to him. His height sitting almost matched my 5'7" standing.

I extended my hand, thankful the music wasn't as loud in the balcony so I didn't have to shout. "I'm Elena. Thank you for the drink, but it really was unnecessary."

He stood. "Elena. Such a beautiful name for a beautiful woman. And such confidence."

At least I succeeded there. My insides turned to rubber as he enfolded my tiny hand in the strong warmth of his. He motioned to the woman sitting next to him, who got up and walked away, glaring at me.

"Please, sit, Elena. Tell me about yourself. How does such a beauty find herself in our humble club? I would surely remember if you had been here before." He sounded anything but humble.

My legs nearly collapsed, forcing me to accept the offer to sit. My steel boned corset prevented me from slumping into the plush couch. I had never experienced true magic, but he certainly seemed to have an otherworldly power contained in all that beauty. I tried to calm myself with deep breaths. I never reacted to men this way. I needed to get a grip on myself, fast. I had a job to do. "Well," I cleared my throat because my voice came out barely audible. "I don't go out very often. But I'm," I didn't want to tell him I was a PI, so quickly thought up an easy lie, "kind of between jobs at the moment and needed to get out of the house."

"You have chosen a wonderful night to come out. It is my fortieth birthday."

"Well, happy birthday, Vittorio. Where's your wife?" Someone as gorgeous as he was either had to be married, or too much of a playboy to ever settle down.

"Hmm," Vittorio murmured, seemingly amused. "I am not

married. I have not found a woman to hold my interest enough for a lifelong commitment. But perhaps that has changed tonight." He eyed me curiously, head slightly tilted to the side.

Oh my word, this god was interested in me. My heart raced. He stared intently into my eyes, and I thought I would faint.

A waitress dropping off a bottle of champagne momentarily distracted Vittorio. Again I reminded myself of my job, wishing I could escape to the bathroom to pull myself together.

Vittorio turned his attention back to me, glass of champagne in hand.

"Thank you, but I don't drink." I longed to accept the glass, to let the soothing affects of the alcohol overtake me. Stressful situations proved most challenging to my sobriety.

"And why is that, mia bella?"

"I've done plenty of drinking to last several lifetimes. I'm done with it."

"That much drinking at your tender age?"

"Tender age? How young do you think I am?"

"Twenty."

"Twenty-five."

"You do not look a day over twenty-one."

"Well thanks. And anyway, I'm much happier when I have full control of my senses.

"But losing control can be such a magical experience." He lightly ran his fingertips from the back of my hand, up my arm, finishing the touch at my neck.

I shivered and my throat went dry.

He smiled, a glint of satisfaction in his eyes. "What can I offer you to drink?"

I cleared my throat, but my voice was still hoarse as I replied. "Just water. Please." I hadn't even noticed my glass was empty.

"As you wish." He nodded to the waitress, who was waiting for his command. That's the only way I can describe it.

She scurried off, abandoning me to Vittorio.

Thankfully, Vittorio turned away from me for a few minutes to grace his other guests with his entrancing conversation skills. It was enough to let me regain some composure yet again. I was exhausted from the emotions racing through my body. What was wrong with me?

I studied the people around me, hoping one might be Courtney, but I saw no one with her facial structure. I sensed this was a very private crowd, and that flashing her picture around would gain me nothing but silence.

All too soon, the waitress returned with my water, and Vittorio again directed his gaze to me.

I couldn't handle any more of my raging hormones, and fished my phone out of my purse to check the time. It was after midnight. "I really should get going."

"May I walk you to your car?"

Oh boy. I really didn't trust myself with him alone. Somehow, I sensed he would not take advantage of me; it was myself I didn't trust. "Thank you for the offer, but I'll be fine." I stood, as did Vittorio. He was more than half a foot taller than me in my high heeled boots, putting him at about 6'6".

"I hope I shall see you again soon, Elena." He reached a hand toward my face, and brushed it down my arm, gently clasping my hand in his. He kissed the back of my hand, turning my body to rubber again.

"I expect you will," I said breathlessly, then fled down the stairs.

CHAPTER THREE

Amazed I made it to the bottom of the stairs without my legs collapsing under me, I pressed my back to the cool stone wall, trying to get control of myself. The bouncer didn't even glance at me, but forcefully stopped a young couple trying to get past him. The craving for a long pull from a bottle of whiskey seized my body stronger than it had since I started detoxing.

The music had softened with a change of DJs. No one on the floor even glanced at me, but on the balcony Vittorio leaned on the railing, watching me, and blew a kiss. I returned a weak smile, then resumed my walk to the bar.

I wanted to calm my racing heart before driving home. After collapsing onto an empty stool, I flagged down the bartender and asked for a glass of water.

"What on earth did you do to him?" she asked when she handed me the glass.

"What? Who?"

"Vittorio. He's completely enamored of you." She grinned.

"How do you know?"

"Felicia, his waitress, told me. She's been working the VIP area for years. His moods have become second nature to her, even though she never sees him outside the club. She said he's never reacted to a woman the way he reacted to you."

Unsure of my ability to form a coherent account of the encounter, I left my reply at, "I don't know."

"You don't know? How can you not? What did you say?" She wiped down the bar while we talked.

I drained my water, desperately wishing it were something - anything - alcoholic. "I just went up and introduced myself to him, thanked him for the drink...that was really it."

"That's it? You must have said or done something extraordinary." She nodded to the balcony. I turned my head and saw Vittorio still watching me.

"I promise you I didn't."

After waiting on a few more customers, she returned with more water.

"What's your name?" I asked.

"Bryn. And you're Elena."

"Gossip travels fast here," I said.

Bryn nodded.

"Alright, Bryn, I'm going to go home and try to figure out what the hell happened to me tonight."

"When will you be back?"

"Who said I'll be back?"

"I don't know a woman in this place who wouldn't want to be in your shoes right now."

I didn't bother trying to lie to her. "Probably sooner than I'd like. I'm not all that sure I like Vittorio's attentions, though."

I walked out to my car in a daze. Somewhere in my back of my head, I knew I needed my wits about me. The Chapel was Midtown, where rent was low but so was security. A few blocks east, you'd be perfectly safe walking back to your car after seeing a musical at The Fox Theater, but stray too far, or visit on the wrong night... I shook my head, trying to figure out where the night had gone wrong. If it had gone wrong at all.

CHAPTER FOUR

Once home, I changed into a black satin nightgown, my breasts and ribs thankful to be out of the corset. The fancy nightgown was one of the few luxuries I allowed myself. I wanted nothing more than to collapse into a deep sleep, but my best friend Kevin burst through the back door, calling my name. Maybe I could pretend to already be asleep. No, he probably saw the light on in my bedroom. "I'm upstairs," I called.

Kevin lived in the other half of the duplex, and had stuck by me through some less than stellar times. He was the only one who did, though I can't figure out why. The duplex may as well have been one house since we both had keys to the other's half.

He stomped up the stairs and sat down at the edge of the bed. "You okay? You're not usually out this late. In fact, you don't usually go out at all."

"Peachy," I said, while washing my face.

"What's wrong? You sound annoyed."

"I'm tired, Kevin." I flopped down on the bed.

"Want me to leave?" He stood and started for the door.

"No, you can stay. I just, well, I guess I'll just tell you. That's the easiest way to explain my mood." I told him about the new case and my night at the club, leaving nothing out, not even my fluttering heart.

He let out a long whistle when I stopped. "So, did you find anything about the girl?"

"That's the problem. I didn't, and I could barely even keep my mind on the reason I was there. I'm more professional than that. I don't know what got into me tonight. Part of me wants nothing more than to lose myself in Vittorio's eyes. The other part wants to run screaming to the other side of the planet. But I have to do this. The Chapel is the most likely place for Courtney to hang out, and the money is too good."

"Good enough that you can buy a new car?"

I'd had my Toyota Corolla with torn seats and windows that wouldn't roll down forever. "Not that good. And anyway, I like my beater. And I like helping you fix it for me when something breaks." Kevin was a mechanic, and without him, I'd never be able to afford to keep my car running. PI work could be damned sporadic at times, making it hard to pay the bills.

"Maybe you can at least pay me to fix it for you now."

"I do pay you. In beer, anyway. And food."

"That I have to cook for you. You'd starve without me." He playfully pushed me.

I pushed him back, almost making him fall off the bed. "There's this newfangled thing called a restaurant. I'd be just fine without you, thank you very much."

"You'd miss me if I wasn't around."

"You know I would." I yawned.

"Why don't you just ask around the club for her?"

"I don't think anyone would answer me."

"You could at least try."

"I have a strange feeling about this case. If Courtney is there, but no one wants to talk to me, I'll never find her. I don't want to let her mother down."

"Why would they lie to you?"

"I don't know, but I intend to find out. Ms. Carmen's comment about the coven put me on edge. I've done some research online, and can't find anything about covens here in St. Louis. At least nothing that looks legit. If she's right, they're very secretive, and I can't risk setting off alarms."

"If you say so," Kevin rolled his eyes.

"If I don't find anything on my own in a few days, I'll start asking around."

"If you need anything, just say the word. Be careful." He hugged me tightly, catching me off guard with the emotional display.

CHAPTER FIVE

I was back at The Chapel, but it wasn't a club. It was the church before the renovation. The pews overflowed with people dressed in their Gothic finest. I floated over the congregation, a detached observer.

Back in my body, I found myself in a little room off the wing of the church. It didn't fit the real life layout of The Chapel, but that's how dreams are sometimes.

Bryn was there with me, her dark tufts of tight curls in contrast to the elegant amethyst gown she wore. It was long and full at the bottom, with a corset bodice that gave her boyish figure just the right curves.

I looked in the mirror; I wore a white gown with a corset top, and tons of tulle under the skirt to make it float out all around me. Elaborate beadwork accented the top. Bryn pinned a veil in my hair, and arranged it over my face. I looked down at my left hand to find a massive diamond on my ring finger. I was getting married, but to whom?

"You're breaking a lot of girls' hearts tonight, Elena," Bryn said.

"I don't know what's going on, but I'm getting out of here." I stormed out the door, only to find myself at the back of the church, with everyone staring at me. Bryn shoved a bouquet of white roses into my sweaty hands and gave me a little push.

Vittorio stood at the altar in a white tuxedo. I was marrying Vittorio?

I walked as slowly as I could, hoping if I delayed reaching the altar long enough, this crazy thing would end, or someone would tell me it was all a joke. Much to my chagrin, they didn't, and I reached the altar.

Vittorio looked at me adoringly and held my hands in his, the bouquet having magically disappeared. I barely heard the minister until he asked me to say the vows. I was in such shock from the whole thing, I said 'I do' before I could stop myself.

The next thing I knew, Vittorio pushed back my veil and kissed me. My body tingled, begging for more, and I thought I would melt right there in his arms.

We walked back down the aisle, my arm through his, as the onlookers threw rose petals at us.

A white carriage pulled by white horses waited outside. Vittorio helped me up into the carriage and kissed me again. "Now, mio amore, we will be together for all eternity."

I woke soaked in sweat. All eternity? What the hell did that mean? I had never dreamed about getting married, much less to someone I had just met. No, I didn't like the way he affected me one bit.

CHAPTER SIX

I arrived at The Chapel a little after 10:00 the next night. The DJ played a softer set of music. I hoped to be able to talk to Bryn and learn something about Courtney. As I walked to the bar my spine tingled; Vittorio watched me from the balcony. I smiled, but continued to the bar. Let him come to me.

Bryn fixed a cranberry and tonic when I sat down. "Hi, Elena. You look like you're breathing easier than when I saw you last."

"I don't know what was wrong with me last night." I shook my head and sighed. The lack of Vittorio's presence was why I breathed easier.

"Uh huh. Vittorio was your problem, and you know it." She glanced at the balcony. "He's been here since we opened at 8:00. Usually he's not here before ten."

"He seemed to have been here quite a while already last night when I went to talk to him."

"That's because it was his birthday. Tonight, he's here for you." She finished mixing a drink and poured it into a glass.

"Did he say that?" He didn't strike me as the kind of guy to be open with his feelings.

"No, but I know things."

"How?" Was she part of this supposed coven?

She delivered the drink, then returned to our conversation. "I'm a woman, silly. Don't you ever just know something by instinct?"

"I guess so." More often than most people did.

"And you're here for him."

"Whatever." I hated to admit even to myself that she was partially right. I liked my life drama-free. Relationships always brought drama.

"Don't lie. I see it in your eyes." She stared at me, hard, daring me to deny it.

"How can it be so obvious when I won't even admit it to myself?"

"Don't worry, he won't know. Unless you tell him. Again, I'm a woman."

"Well, he can come to me. I'm not chasing him. I can wait all night." As I said that, the air energized.

"Looks like you won't have to," Julia said. She lowered her voice. "You really did a number on him. He never approaches a woman. He doesn't have to." She turned away to wash some glasses that looked already clean.

"Elena." My body tightened at that voice. "I am pleased to see you again so soon. I hope you are well?"

I had been until his voice turned my bones to rubber again. But I would be strong, unattainable. "I am. And you?" There. My voice didn't shake at all.

He caressed my skin from neck to hand, ending with a gentle kiss on the back of my hand as he had the night before, sending shivers through my body. From the corner of my eye I saw Bryn watching us.

"I am splendid." His gaze held mine, unwavering.

I took a sip of my drink. "Glad to hear it." Again, voice even. Point for me.

"Would you give me the pleasure of your company upstairs?"

"Well, I was in the middle of a conversation with Bryn, but I'd be happy to join you in a while."

I caught a flicker of disappointment in his eyes, but it was gone an instant later. "I hope you are not too long, but I wouldn't dream of tearing you away from girl talk." He smiled, and any part of me that wasn't yet rubber melted. He nodded to Bryn, who nodded back curtly, and walked towards the stairs.

I watched him walk away. The crowd parted for him. No joke. I forced my gaze back to Bryn when he disappeared up the stairs. "Ho-ly shit," I muttered.

"You can say that again," Bryn agreed, and then left me to my thoughts while she helped other customers.

I didn't want to be left with my X-rated thoughts just then.

CHAPTER SEVEN

The bouncer barely even looked at me as I passed him. I stopped at the top of the stairs to ensure my composure was firmly in place and found Vittorio deep in conversation with another man. I glanced at the crowd; the way they drooled over Vittorio, male and female alike, made me sick. He was only human, after all. Right, I'd have to remember that. Only human. I had to remember why I was here - to find a woman's runaway daughter, not to lust after some Italian hot-body. My gaze drifted back to Vittorio and stopped there. I realized I was no better than anyone else besotted by him.

As if he heard my thoughts, Vittorio looked over to me. He stood in one liquid movement and glided toward me.

My heart raced. Crap.

"Elena. How long have you been standing there?"

"Only a minute." I shifted from one foot to the other, uncomfortable with my fluttering heart.

"Sorry to keep you waiting. Samuel and I were talking business."

"I don't want to interrupt," I said.

"Please do. He's a dreadful bore. Please, come sit with me." He took my hand and led me back to the love seat. Samuel stood, nodded toward me, and left.

"Bryn said you were here early tonight."

"Yes, business. It's a convenient meeting place for Samuel and me, as we have a shared office up here." He gestured to the room in the back. "But he doesn't know when to stop. He's all work, no play."

"Why do you have an office here?"

"I co-own this establishment, along with Samuel. I mainly provide the finances; he handles the business side of things."

"Oh," I said, picking at the skin around my nails, then mentally kicking myself for being so unintelligible.

"You look radiant tonight, Elena," Vittorio said, changing the subject. Again he kissed the back of my hand, but thankfully without the rest of the touch on my arm this time. "Did you sleep well last night?"

"Well enough, aside from some interesting dreams." Now why did I say that?

Vittorio raised an eyebrow. "Oh?"

"I don't really remember them," I lied. "They were very active dreams, though. The kind that leave you more tired when you wake up than when you went to sleep."

"Ah yes, I know exactly the type. I am sorry you did not sleep well." His brow furrowed.

"It's not your fault." At least not directly. Or so I thought. "I slept well enough, it just wasn't restful. But I had nothing to do today anyway, so it's alright."

"What do you do with your time?"

"Read, mostly. I jog a couple miles every day." That much was true. "I suppose I should get a job eventually."

"What do you want to do?" He took a sip of wine.

I shrugged. "Maybe apply at a bookstore. I do love books."

"And hanging out at Goth clubs alone. Surely you have a boyfriend who could escort you?" The words were casual, but his carefully neutral face showed he worried the answer would be yes.

"No. I don't date much. What about you? Tell me about yourself."

"I work with Samuel at Porter Enterprises. I am the Vice President of Human Resources. His father owns the company. When I'm not here or working, I, too, like to read. You should come see my library sometime."

"Maybe when I know you a little better." If I rarely dated, I went to strange men's homes even less. "What else?"

"I also enjoy bird watching."

"Bird watching?"

"Yes, is that so unbelievable?" He leaned toward me.

"No, it's just not a common hobby. At least not with anyone I know." Unthinking, I leaned slightly toward him.

"But you know me." He took my hand in his.

"Well, now I do, but I don't, really. I'm merely acquainted with you." I stumbled over my words, trying to maintain my composure.

"You are particular." He wiped a bead of sweat from his temple. I hadn't thought the balcony wasn't that warm. "We'll have to do something about changing that, will we not?" His words held a hundred meanings, but as he touched my face, my body only recognized one.

I stood clumsily. "I need to use the restroom. I'll be right back." I hated being rude, but couldn't help myself. I had to get away, even if just for a few minutes.

I was thankful to find the restroom unoccupied. Sitting on the cool porcelain lid of the toilet, I held my head in my hands. What the hell was wrong with me? Why did I react to Vittorio this strongly? I wanted to slap myself, but a handprint on my face wouldn't be becoming. I had a job to do, I reminded myself yet again. I tried to shut my hormones down, but settled for my heartbeat slowing just a bit.

The waitress dropped off a cranberry and tonic just as I returned. "You looked like you needed a drink. Do not worry, no alcohol. I did not forget," he said.

"Thanks." I sniffed the drink to be sure, half wishing he lied.

"Now where were we?" His voice held promise of things I didn't want to contemplate.

"Bird watching," I said hoarsely.

"Ah yes. You were surprised at my hobby. Have you ever watched a bird?"

"Not really."

"You should sometime. They are fascinating creatures. Not so fascinating as some, however." He stared intently into my eyes as he said this.

I swallowed hard.

"Quite beautiful, too. Would you care to join me sometime?"

I couldn't think straight. What was he asking me? I didn't know, but said yes anyway, immediately regretting it.

"Wonderful. How about the day after tomorrow then?"

"So soon?" I couldn't make sense of the conversation.

"Why not?"

Why not indeed? I couldn't come up with an answer. "Um." Surely I had some excuse why not. I couldn't even make one up though. My brain was mush. "Okay." I had to get out of there.

"Shall I pick you up at 6:00 then? Bird-watching is best done early in the morning."

He already haunted my dreams. I didn't want him haunting me in wakefulness. But didn't guys usually pick girls up for a first date? I gave him my address and he tapped it into his phone.

"Now, it is getting late. May I walk you to your car?"

I didn't want to be rude, so accepted.

He stood with catlike grace, and held out his hand to help me up. He bent his arm at his side, and I looped mine through his, feeling very old fashioned.

The instant I did, I wished I hadn't. The world swam. It was the most contact we had shared, the length of his body pressed lightly to mine. The warmth of his touch overwhelmed me. It was as if his aura tried to meld with mine.

"Are you alright, Elena?"

I shook my head and took a few deep breaths. "Yes, I'm just tired. And I think I've had too much cranberry juice the past few days. It messes with my body if I drink too much of it." That was the most pathetic excuse I'd ever made.

He didn't press the issue, simply looked thoughtful.

The dizziness passed as he loosened his grasp on my arm, putting a few inches between us, and we started for the stairs.

Tired, my body not working with my brain, I welcomed the cool night air I otherwise would have shivered against. I felt weak, and hoped I wasn't getting sick. That would be a bad way to start an investigation, but if I could blame all this on being sick, I'd almost prefer that over the alternative.

"Do you believe in magic?" I blurted before I could make sense of my thoughts.

"The world is full of mysterious things. Why do you ask?" It wasn't really an answer, but at least he hadn't ridiculed my silly question.

"No reason, forget it. I'm just tired."

"I shall see you the day after tomorrow at six then?" Vittorio asked for confirmation.

"Yes."

He stroked my cheek, and oh so gently tipped my chin up. His lips brushed against mine, the barest of kisses, so light I might have imagined it.

Feeling my legs about to give out, I sat down in my car, thankful I had already opened the door, hoping he hadn't noticed my weakness. "See you then."

"I will be counting the hours." He bowed slightly from the waist, and then walked away.

Was this guy for real? Unfortunately for me, he was.

CHAPTER EIGHT

"Kevin, I'm scared." I went straight to his half of the duplex when I got home that night and flopped on his couch.

"Then call Ms. Carmen and tell her you can't take the case after all."

"I can't do that. I need the money." I stood, full of restless energy.

"You know I'll help you out if you need it. I don't want to see you get hurt."

"Vittorio wouldn't hurt me. He's a gentleman." I paced Kevin's living room.

"But you said you're scared." He didn't put the game controller down, but I knew I had his full attention. He could play video games in his sleep.

"Not like that. I'm scared of the way I'm feeling. I've never been affected like this by a man. It's like, this is going to sound stupid, but you know those movies where the handsome vampire uses his powers to seduce the beautiful young maiden?"

"Yeah." Kevin covered his mouth, stifling a laugh.

"I told you it was stupid." I sat back down on the couch, embarrassed for even comparing Vittorio to a vampire. But I didn't know how else to explain it. I didn't date much, and a pretty face never impressed me. But Vittorio did. Why?

"Vampires aren't real, Elena." Kevin gestured to emphasize his point.

"I know that. But I don't understand why I'm so attracted to him. I mean, he's gorgeous, yeah, but it's not just that. I can't explain it."

"I'll say it again. Call Ms. Carmen and tell her you can't work the case."

"And I'll say it again, I can't do that. She's really worried about her daughter. I won't let her down."

Kevin sighed.

"I just need someone to talk to, Kevin. I'm not backing out of this case. If I can't talk to you about this without you jumping all over me, tell me now."

Kevin opened his mouth.

I cut him off. "And before you say anything, think carefully. You know how rarely I say I need anything from anyone."

"I was going to say, I'm here for you. I'm sorry, Elena. I worry about you, but if you want me to shut up and simply listen, I will."

"Good, because that is what I need. That, and sleep, though I'm not sure sleep will be possible."

I spent the next day researching Vittorio, Samuel, and Porter Enterprises, having regained my wits and skill as a PI.

Vittorio had immigrated from Italy nearly twenty years ago. Bryn hadn't been exaggerating when she'd said he was full-blooded Italian. According to a news article announcing his promotion to Vice President of Human Resources, he had worked hard to gain his position in the company, and earned every dollar of his considerable wealth. He was a social butterfly, and repeatedly made both St. Louis' and Missouri's "Most Eligible Bachelors" lists, but I could find no details about his past in Italy.

I ran a background check on him, which showed nothing out of the ordinary. Aside from a few speeding and parking tickets, he was an upstanding citizen. He obtained his citizenship ten years ago.

Samuel's background check was more interesting. There was absolutely nothing on his police record, not even a parking ticket. It was too clean. News articles hinted at a checkered youth -

partying, pot and the like - so I assumed his father had lawyers to expunge any trace of wrongdoing from his son's record. People with checkered youths and lots of money rarely turned out to be saints, as Samuel's record showed him to be.

I was about to give up when one last article caught my eye. It showed a color photograph of Samuel and a gorgeous, very Gothic woman. The caption read, "Samuel Porter and companion Elizabeth Hardgrave entering the St. Louis Art Museum for the premiere of the Caribbean Art Showcase." I wondered if this was the same Elizabeth Ms. Carmen had referred to. I read the article, dated six months ago, to discover the event wasn't just an opening of a special exhibit but also a fundraiser to help expand the museum.

My jaw dropped at the name of the museum curator. Alexis Carmen. Could this be a coincidence? Doubtful.

I called Ms. Carmen.

"Elena, have you found my daughter?" she asked as soon as I said my name.

"No, but I have a question for you. Do you know someone named Samuel Porter?"

"The name sounds familiar." She paused. "Yes, I met him once, about six months ago. He was at a fundraiser at the art museum. I work there. He was very interested in a map I lent for the display. He wanted to buy it, but I would never sell it. He threw out some exorbitant numbers, but I don't need the money, and refused."

"What was the map of?" I asked.

"It shows the route of one of Ponce de Leon's lesser known expeditions, and supposedly the real location of the Fountain of Youth."

"The real location?"

"Most legends say it is in Florida, but other stories put it somewhere around the Yucatan Peninsula and the Gulf of Honduras."

I wrote that down. "Did you meet the woman he was with that night?"

"No, but I saw him with her later in the evening."

"Do you know her name?"

"No, I'd never seen her before and haven't since. What does this have to do with Courtney?"

"Ms. Carmen, are you telling me you didn't read the articles about the premiere?"

"I glanced at them, but I'm not interested in what reporters have to say about my museum." She said reporters as if it were a dirty word.

She sounded sincere, so I let it go. "Her name is Elizabeth Hardgrave. Do you think it could be the same woman you overheard your daughter mention?"

"I don't know, now that you mention it, she did look Goth, yet more elegant than my daughter dresses. It could be, but I really can't be certain."

"Thank you, Ms. Carmen. I won't take any more of your time right now."

CHAPTER NINE

I decided on black jeans and a fitted royal purple T-shirt for the bird watching outing. I kept my makeup simple with black eyeliner and deep red lipstick, hoping Vittorio would be less likely to kiss me if my lips were painted. I was probably wrong, but a girl could dream.

I sipped my third cup of coffee when a knock on the door startled me. I opened it to find Vittorio, exactly on time.

He wore a pair of dark jeans and an untucked black T-shirt. It was plain, but still managed to look expensive. I wanted to touch it to feel what it was made of, but knew that was a bad idea if I wanted to maintain control over myself.

Had it not been for the long, thick hair he had pulled back into a braid, he would have looked normal; well, as normal as a man that tall with the face of a god can look, that is. As had become the norm, my heart skipped a beat or five when I saw him.

"Elena." He greeted me with the now customary arm stroke and kiss on the back of the hand. "Even dressed down you look stunning."

My face burned. "Thank you." I looked down shyly, a foreign movement to my body. I had never been shy.

"Are you ready for your first bird watching lesson?"

"You better believe it." At least I sounded more confident than I felt.

We walked outside to a freshly waxed black Ferrari California.

He opened the passenger door and held my hand as I sank down into the supple black leather seats, inhaling the warm scent of leather that enfolded my body. I sighed contentedly. This was so much nicer than my beat up Corolla. "I bet this is fun to drive during the winter," I said.

"I have a Mercedes G550 to get through bad weather."

Of course he did. Why would I have thought he only had the one car like us mortals?

Vittorio started the car and classical music floated from the speakers, meshing with the purr of the engine. "Do you like *Faust*?" he asked.

"What?"

"Charles Gounod's opera *Faust*."

"I've never been a fan of opera."

"Why is that, mia bella?" He turned his whole body toward me.

We hadn't even pulled away from the curb and my hormones took control of my body. I focused on the memory that started my distaste for classical music, wrapped it around me as a shield to block out Vittorio's gaze. It worked. I'd have to remember hate was a powerful shield. "My grandmother listened to it constantly. Whenever I visited her, she made me listen to it, grilled me about how it made me feel, what I thought it was about. I didn't care, and I had no idea what they were singing about in a foreign language. She smacked me whenever I said something rude about opera, which made me hate it even more."

"Will you try listening to a little bit with me, and if you still do not like it, I will turn on whatever music you like?"

"Why do you want me to listen to it so badly?"

"I have a feeling you will like it, if only you give it a chance. I adore opera, and want to share it with you. I want to share everything with you."

Everything? His eyes bored into me, pleading. My pulse raced, hatred of my grandmother long gone. How could I say no? I couldn't say yes either; my throat was too dry. I nodded.

"Thank you," he said, as he lightly touched my cheek, sending tingles through my whole body. That one touch should not be so

31

sensual.

Vittorio narrated the opera while driving at high speeds through winding country roads after we drove west away from the city. I watched as he drove with confidence, admiring his features and his deep, rhythmic voice. Every once in a while he would turn to look at me, and smile.

I focused on Vittorio while he narrated. I needed to be able to control myself around him. If I could watch him under a controlled circumstance such as this and keep my feelings in check, I'd have a start to build upon in less controllable situations. Such as when there was less than a foot of space separating us. And if I was really lucky, even when he touched me, or kissed me.

At the end of the hour, by some miracle, I was able to control my heart every time he smiled at me. Perhaps it was because there was a full foot of space between our seats. Whatever the reason, for the first time since I had met him, I could concentrate.

By the time he pulled off the side of the winding road and parked the car, I realized I no longer hated opera. Perhaps it was simply the fact that he was the one narrating, but I found myself enjoying the music and wanting to hear more.

He came around to my side to help me out of the low vehicle.

My heart sped as he rested his hand lightly on the small of my back, but my legs remained firmly beneath me; a vast improvement from the other night. He held my hand as we walked through the trees. The sound of chirping birds and leaves rustling in the breeze filled the air. We eventually reached a clearing with a stream lined with bushes at the opposite side. Vittorio stopped and pulled a thin blanket out of his backpack.

Seeing Vittorio outside of the club in jeans and a T-shirt carrying a backpack was an odd sight indeed. His long thick hair and perfect face didn't fit the image of rugged nature man; yet somehow it seemed right and reasonable. He was the type of man who would look at ease in any situation.

Vittorio gestured for me to sit, then sat dangerously close to me, unpacking a pair of binoculars. For once, his attention was not focused on me. I was surprised to find myself feeling slighted. Then he drew in his breath, pointed across the field and handed the binoculars to me. "Do you see those blue jays over there?"

I searched, but couldn't find them.

He leaned closer to me, gently put his arm around my shoulders, and helped me aim the binoculars in the right direction. I almost lost all focus at his touch until I found the birds, flitting around a bush by the stream. They were beautiful, and I didn't mind that his attention was on them instead of me.

"Wait here. I'll be right back," Vittorio said after some time of bird watching.

"Where are you going?"

"Relax. I have a surprise in the car. I'll only be a minute." He kissed the back of my hand.

True to his word, Vittorio returned with a basket. Very quaint.

"You must be getting hungry. I know I am." His voice held heat that alluded to more than lunch.

Any control I had mustered over the course of the morning fled and my mouth went dry.

I tried to swallow. "Well, now that you mention it, I am." The last two words came out far more breathy than I intended.

He unpacked sandwiches, fruit, and a bottle of wine. "Did you forget I don't drink?" I asked.

"Of course not. I haven't forgotten a word that has passed your lips. This is sparkling grape juice. I thought it a good finishing touch since I cannot share my Italian wines with you."

I read the label and found he was telling the truth. Silly me. I bit into a sandwich realizing the extent of my hunger. My nerves hadn't allowed me to have more than coffee earlier. The fruit tasted sweet and juicy. I inhaled the food in an unladylike manner, but didn't care. If Vittorio wanted me, he could have me in all my starving glory. When we finished eating, he packed up and we walked back to the car.

"Would you do me the honor of joining me at the club tonight?"

"I'd love to," I said honestly. "What time should I meet you there?"

"I would like it if you would come with me, as my date."

"Well, I'll need to go home and change."

"Do not worry about that. Come home with me." I looked at him in alarm. "Now, now, where is your mind taking you? In case you have not noticed, I am a gentleman." He grinned at me. "I will take you shopping, buy you a new gown."

Gown? Who said 'gown' these days?

"You can shower and dress at my place. You will have your privacy. I simply wish to enter the club with you on my arm tonight."

As he looked at me pleadingly, his crystal clear emerald eyes boring into my soul, I couldn't refuse. As soon as I said yes, I mentally kicked myself. Why would I do that? Young women should not go to the homes of strange, older men.

I didn't like the conflicted thoughts in my head the past few days. I couldn't explain them. However, I still sensed Vittorio meant me no harm, so I stuck with my decision, for better or worse.

CHAPTER TEN

I had driven past, but never stopped in the store on South Grand Avenue filled with the most exquisite Goth club wear imaginable. Unlike many girls, I detested window-shopping. What was the point of drooling over something you couldn't afford?

Elegant Gothic and Victorian style dresses filled some racks, while others contained leather and PVC clothes. Fishnet and lace were abundant throughout the store, as was silver jewelry. When I looked at a price tag of one dress that read $2000, I turned to leave. "I can't afford this, Vittorio."

"Do not fret, I told you I would buy you a gown."

"I can't accept something like this from you."

"I insist."

"No, really. I barely know you. I can't."

He almost looked hurt. "Elena, please. My job provides more income than I know what to do with. I do not say that to brag, simply to illustrate the point that if I wish to buy a beautiful woman an expensive gown, there is no reason for her to turn me down."

Glancing around the store, I saw several items I would love to own. "You're not going to give me a choice, are you?"

"I would never dream of taking choices away from you."

I didn't like it, but grudgingly accepted his offer. What would it hurt to have a really nice gown anyway? "Alright, I'll let you buy me a dress."

"Thank you," he said, and sounded sincere.

I didn't understand what was going on, but filed it in my brain to ponder when I was alone. Why was it so important that I allow him to buy me a dress?

I looked through racks of dresses, skirts, and corsets, unable to choose just one.

Vittorio came to my rescue with an item that could only be called a gown, never a mere dress, and asked if I would try it on.

The gown was surprisingly simple. The top was a black corset connected to a long, flowing skirt with a short train, and made of a fine satin. Royal purple was woven throughout in the form of a shimmering thread. I felt like a princess, and dared not look at the price tag.

The saleslady brought me shoes with a four-inch heel that matched the purple in the dress, and suggested black lace panties, silk stockings, and a garter belt to match. I wasn't sure about the matching undergarment set; no one would see it. She insisted they would help me feel sexy, even if no one saw, so I accepted.

When I changed back into my street clothes, I told Vittorio I loved it. "I'm going to wait outside while you pay. I do not want to know what this costs," I said firmly.

After a light dinner, we went to Vittorio's mansion. It was old, built of stone, and looked like a European fortress. I'd often driven past the mansions lining Forsyth Avenue, wondering what they looked like inside. Any home directly across from Forest Park would be expensive, but I couldn't imagine what these cost. I expected to find gaudy, ostentatious furniture and decorations inside. A clean, modern decorating style surprised me. The rooms were not sparse, but with fifteen-foot ceilings, seemed open and airy.

Our footsteps echoed on marble floors as he led me to the guest suite. A few paintings hung on the walls, but not so many that the hall appeared cluttered. One in particular caught my attention. It was a crow in boots walking through a barren field. A dead tree loomed in the background.

"That's an interesting painting," I said.

"It's one of my favorites. It is *Krahe*, by Rudi Hurzlmeier."

"It's sad, but kind of whimsical at the same time." We admired the painting side by side for a few moments.

We finally reached the guest suite at the end of the long hallway. It was a large, tastefully decorated bedroom with mahogany furniture. The bedding was midnight blue with traces of silver throughout and looked inviting, even though I wasn't tired. A freestanding full length mirror stood next to the dresser. The bathroom was the size of the entire first floor of my duplex. A Jacuzzi tub that looked as if it could hold four people sat in one corner, a giant shower in another. Makeup, shampoo, lotion - the works - lined up on the double vanity lining one wall

"Do you make a habit of hosting women at your home?" I asked, hating the jealous tone I heard in my voice.

"Elena, please do not be upset. I do not. When you agreed to come back with me, I sent my assistant a message asking her to pick these things up for you. You are a rare exception in my life. Bryn must have talked about me, and I will not deny that it is not difficult for me to keep myself, how shall I say, occupied. But now that I have met you, I wish to have no other women in my life - if I would be so lucky as to have you in my life."

"Well," I started, almost stunned into wordlessness. "I don't usually rush into things, with men or in any other area of my life. I hardly know you. But we'll see where this leads."

"That is all I can ask. Now, I shall leave you to prepare for the evening." He swept out of the room.

Is this guy for real? I asked myself for the umpteenth time. I'd heard of love at first sight, but wasn't it usually silly teenage girls who fell for that sort of nonsense? You can't love someone, much less know that you want them in your life forever, when you've only known them a few short days. Can you?

Then again, I was having some pretty crazy thoughts myself. Dreams of marriage, being ridiculously attracted to a near stranger, the inability to control my thoughts and keep my head out of the clouds whenever Vittorio was near.

Whenever he was near. I felt more in control of myself now that he wasn't in the room with me. Was it magic? I believed in the possibility. Just because there was no proof of magic didn't mean it wasn't real. My job had taught me to keep an open mind.

When I finished showering, I heard a knock at the bathroom door.

"Miss, would you like help with your hair?" a female voice said.

I hadn't planned on doing anything with it. I wasn't very good at hairstyles. "Um, alright." I opened the door, wearing a robe I found in the bathroom, and a tall, pretty woman of about thirty with honey blonde hair and a flawless complexion came in.

"I'm Sarah, Vittorio's assistant."

What else did she help him with, I wondered? The thought must have shown on my face.

"It's all business between us. Please don't be jealous."

I was usually so good at hiding my thoughts. What was it about Vittorio that left me so open and raw? "I'm sorry. Thank you for offering to help. Whenever I try to do anything fancier than a blow dry, I end up looking like the Bride of Frankenstein."

An hour later my hair was beautifully swept up on top of my head, half of it left trailing down my back in thick curls. My makeup was done and I was dressed and ready to go. I felt beautiful. I had to admit the saleslady was right about the matching undergarments. They made me feel incredibly sexy, and knowing I looked good through and through gave me an extra boost of confidence.

Sarah led me downstairs to a study where Vittorio sat reading an old, leather-bound book. He stood when I entered the room. He was richly dressed in a gothic tuxedo with a hint of shine. A deep purple satin shirt matched the detail in my dress. His long hair flowed freely down his back, and a silver ring with a deep purple stone glinted on his finger.

I caught my breath, stunned by his beauty. Surely I was in a dream. No real man was this perfect.

Vittorio seemed equally as stunned by me. He paused and stared at me for a moment, then glided toward me and took both my hands in his. "Elena, you are stunning. You shall be the envy of everyone at The Chapel tonight."

I regained a bit of composure. "What's the special occasion? Why are we so dressed up?"

"Nothing special. I am only proud to have you with me." He kissed the back of my hand. "Shall we go?"

I nodded. There had to be some reason for all this elegance. I followed Vittorio to his car, eager to learn more.

CHAPTER ELEVEN

Entering The Chapel on Vittorio's arm, I felt like a movie star, but there was no red carpet, and no photographers. Everyone watched as we entered. Stunned by the attention, I didn't have a chance to feel weak from Vittorio's closeness. We ascended the stairs to the balcony, and settled onto a love seat while Felicia took our drink order. I opted for a Coke this time.

"You are gorgeous, mia bella," Vittorio breathed into my ear as he nuzzled my neck.

I couldn't breathe, couldn't think. His lips lightly touched me, and suddenly it was just the two of us, alone in the world. The warmth of his body close to mine erased awareness of anything else; even the seat on which I sat disappeared. My heart hammered; my breath came fast and shallow. That one touch was better than any sexual encounter I had ever experienced. I didn't understand it, but that slight amount of contact left my body screaming for more.

The sound of Vittorio saying my name brought me back to my senses, but I was confused, as if I was coming out of a dream. "What?"

"Are you alright? Shall I take you home?"

I shook my head to clear it. "No, I'm alright, just a little dizzy. Must be all the fresh air from today or something. I just need something to drink." I looked around, and saw that our drinks sat on the table near the love seat. I reached for mine, and took a long drink through the straw.

"If you feel ill and want to leave, please say so."

"Thank you, but no." Vittorio looked at me, brow furrowed,

and I wondered what was going through his mind.

We talked with some of the other people around us, and I was thankful to not have Vittorio's full attention. I looked around, wondering if any of the young girls were Courtney or Miriam, hoping to see Elizabeth, but could hardly focus. I don't know how much time had passed when Samuel appeared next to him. "You seem quite enamored of your new plaything, Vittorio," he said, gesturing toward me.

That brought me fully back to my senses.

"Excuse me?" I stood up, fists clenched at my sides. "I am no one's plaything. Just who do you think you are?"

"Surely Vittorio told you we are business partners?" Samuel said, head held high.

"Surely he did, but that gives you no right to be rude and condescending to me. You don't know the first thing about me."

Vittorio stood. "Samuel, I expect you to apologize to Elena. You have no right to be so rude to her."

"Apologize to your latest toy? I don't think so," Samuel said.

"I hope you don't think I am your plaything," I said to Vittorio.

"Of course not. You are every bit my equal, and a strong, independent woman." He looked at Samuel. "You will apologize."

"You think so?" Samuel asked and raised an eyebrow.

"Yes. I do," Vittorio said through clenched teeth.

"Why the hell should I? She is no different any other tramp you traipse through here with."

I slapped him. My father's mistress had called me a tramp every day before I ran away from home for good. I hadn't stood up to her, but I damn well would stand up to Samuel.

Everyone turned to see what the sound was. A look between horror and amusement graced Vittorio's face as a red handprint blossomed on Samuel's cheek. He stepped between Samuel and me, facing me, his back to Samuel.

"Elena, please. I think you have made your point."

"Obviously I haven't. I want Samuel to apologize." Through my anger, I found myself able to stare into his eyes and remain unaffected. I felt hostility in mine. Did he really expect me to stand there and take this?

Apparently not, for a look of resolve replaced the amusement. He turned toward Samuel. "Samuel, you will apologize to Elena. I told you; she is not just another piece of arm candy. As far as I am concerned, she is the only woman in the world. And she is her own woman. I would never dream of thinking of her as less than an equal to myself. You, on the other hand, may not be such an equal as I once thought."

Whatever Samuel saw in his face seemed to frighten him.

"I'm sorry, Elena," Samuel said, looking down at the floor.

"Look at me when you apologize."

He looked at me, eyes wide and frightened. "I'm sorry. Please forgive my rudeness." He pleaded with his eyes.

I wondered what Vittorio would do to him if I didn't accept his apology. "Apology accepted."

"Elena, would you excuse Samuel and me for a few minutes? I think I need to have a discussion with him."

"Sure. I'm going to go talk to Bryn." I started to walk away before he gently caught my arm. The touch was slight, but the energy was enough to stop me in my tracks. I turned back to him.

"I am sorry for this." He leaned down and brushed his lips against mine. I almost fell. I grabbed him for support, and he wrapped his arm around my waist. His strength was all that held me up. My body was fully pressed against him in his grip.

"This isn't helping." I didn't want him to know what an effect he had on me, but had no choice at that moment. I lay my head against his chest, weak, but that made it even worse. I took deep breaths, feeling as if I was drunk.

He nodded to Felicia, who rushed over. "Felicia, help Elena downstairs. She's feeling a bit faint."

Felicia wrapped an arm around my waist, and I draped an arm

over her shoulders, trying to act as if we were close friends, but knowing the act fooled no one. I hated showing this much vulnerability in front of so many people, especially Samuel, but had no choice unless I wanted to collapse to the ground, which would be even more embarrassing.

We slowly made our way down the stairs. "Shall I help you into the restroom?" Felicia asked.

"No, just to the bar, please. Thank you. I must have eaten something bad today. I'm so embarrassed."

"It's okay, don't be. Vittorio has that affect on people."

I looked at her in alarm. What did she mean by that?

"He is extremely handsome," she said.

"Yes, he is, but men, handsome or not, do not affect me like this. I think I'm just coming down with something."

CHAPTER TWELVE

I plopped unceremoniously onto a barstool. "Good lord, girl, what happened to you? You're white as a ghost," Bryn shouted over the music.

"Vittorio happened to me," I said, surprising myself with my bluntness.

"Ah," she said knowingly. "I've seen women swoon for him before, but you look like death warmed over. Must have been some make-out session," she grinned.

"He barely kissed me." I lay my head down on the bar, hoping to avoid any sticky spots, but not really caring. A minute later I felt someone brushing my hair off my neck and laying a cool washcloth on it. I looked around to see Bryn behind me. "Thanks."

"What's going on? This isn't a normal reaction to hormones?" Bryn asked.

It was easier to talk over the music with her right next to me. "I wish I knew. I should probably just go home and never show my face here again. It might be safer that way."

"You won't do that."

"How do you know?"

"Remember? I'm a woman." She grinned at me. "Tell me about that dress. You look fabulous!"

I blushed. "Vittorio bought it for me. I feel like a princess."

"You look like one. I'll say it again; you really did a number on him." She looked up to the balcony, and I turned to look when I saw the curious expression on her face. Vittorio and Samuel appeared to be having a heated discussion. "Wonder what they're arguing about."

"Probably me."

"Did Samuel put the moves on you? Man, he sure would be stupid to do that in front of Vittorio."

"No, he did something even dumber. He insulted me. Called me Vittorio's plaything. Then I slapped him."

"Wow. You've got guts. People try to impress him almost as much as Vittorio, sometimes more." Bryn looked at the growing number of customers at the bar. "I've got to get back to work. Looks like you should get back to Vittorio." She gestured to the balcony, from where he now watched me.

I wanted to ask her what she meant by people trying to impress Samuel, but didn't, as she was busy mixing drinks. Was he part of this mysterious coven Ms. Carmen told me about? I really hoped my hormones would shut the hell up soon so I could focus on the case.

Returning upstairs, I was relieved to find Samuel nowhere in sight, though Vittorio looked angry. He was alone on the love seat, so I sat next to him and rested my hand on his arm, subtly testing my reaction to him. I was pleased to feel only a slight tingle down my spine. "Are you okay?"

He turned to me and smiled. "I should be the one asking you that. I am fine. Samuel and I often have disagreements."

"That looked like more than a disagreement."

"Yes, well, I think he understands now what you mean to me. How are you my dear?"

"A little shaky," I admitted. I was beyond the point of acting cool and aloof toward him. My episode earlier had destroyed any chance of hiding his effect on me.

"Interesting," he murmured.

"What's that?"

Vittorio looked into my eyes for a moment, then leaned in and kissed me gently. I panicked, but as soon as his lips touched mine, I lost all sense of time and space again. When he pulled away, I sank back into the corner of the couch, as far away from him as I could get without standing up, which wasn't an option on my rubbery legs. I couldn't take this. "Vittorio, I want an honest answer from you. Why do you affect me this way? Did you drug my drinks?" Had I really been that stupid?

"I would never dream of doing such a thing to anyone, especially you. You are far too important," he said, cupping my face in his hand.

I almost believed him.

"I have a guess, but am not yet certain. Perhaps we should go someplace a little more private to discuss this. Would you return to my home with me?"

"No offense, but that sounds a little too private." I tried to sink further away and into the couch. Maybe I could simply disappear.

"You have my word; I will not take advantage of you. I will not even touch you if you wish."

"That's the problem. I want you to touch me, yet I'm afraid."

"Do you want me to kiss you?" Sweat shone on his forehead.

"Yes," I breathed.

"Then you have my word; I shall do no more than kiss you tonight."

"Even that might be more than I can handle." Why did I admit that to him? I must have been more tired that I realized.

"I promise to take care of you Elena. We have just met, but already you mean the world to me."

"Why? You don't even know me." He sounded sincere, and I felt guilty for not being honest with him about my profession.

"Please come home with me. I will try to explain everything there." His eyes bored into mine, as if he could see right through to my soul.

I didn't like any of this, but I had to know what was going on. I had to get over this strange attraction to him so I could focus on the investigation. I sighed. "All right. But first I want you to tell me why you were so determined to buy me this dress. Why was it so damned important?"

"I wanted you to arrive with me to make a sort of statement that I'm no longer available."

"Why would me coming with you say that?"

"I always come on my own. I may leave with someone else, but I do not bring dates here. The people who matter understood what that meant. I meant it when I said I wish to have no other woman in my life."

Vittorio's was a world very different from mine. I still didn't quite understand, but he seemed to be telling the truth. And I really wanted to leave, so I accepted his answer and let him help me out to the Ferrari.

CHAPTER THIRTEEN

When we got back to Vittorio's house, Sarah helped me into the guest suite. "Are there some sweats or something I could change into?"

"Of course, miss." She turned to leave the room.

"Please, call me Elena."

"Of course, Elena. I'll be right back." She returned with the softest sweat suit I had ever felt.

"I'm sorry it's so big, but it's Vittorio's and is all I could find. He doesn't make a habit of hosting women here." She held up the deep maroon outfit and handed it to me.

"Did he pay you to say that?"

"Of course not." Her hand went to her chest in offense.

"I'm sorry, Sarah. I was trying to make a joke. I believe you, and God only knows why, I believe him."

"Vittorio is a man of honor. He doesn't seem to fit in our time period."

"That's for sure." When she left, I put on the sweats, pulling the drawstring to the pants as tight as it would go. I rolled up the legs, and pushed the sleeves up my arms, but I still swam in them.

A few minutes later, Vittorio knocked on the door. I let him in, and he sat in an armchair next to the bed. I sat on the bed, as far from him as possible. I wanted to wrap myself around him, so thought more distance was better.

"What the hell is happening to me?"

"Right to the point," he said softly.

"Don't mess with me, Vittorio. I don't like feeling so out of control. I want to understand what's going on." I hugged my knees to my chest.

"Forgive me. I will explain the best I can, not fully understanding it myself, but you must keep an open mind." He paused. "Do you believe in magic?"

I snorted. "You're kidding, right?"

His serious face told me he was not.

"I guess I believe it's possible, but I've never experienced it."

"What if I told you magic was real?"

"If you told me you were using vampire powers on me, I'd probably believe you."

That elicited a chuckle. "I am no vampire. Perhaps I should demonstrate." He stood, walked across the room, and turned off the light.

I felt him stand next to the bed. Then I saw a faint glow near him. I hadn't seen him carrying a flashlight. The glow grew brighter, and as my eyes adjusted to the light, I saw an orb in his hand.

"Nice trick. But it's just a fancy flashlight, right?"

"Do you think so? Try to take it from me."

I knelt on the bed and carefully moved closer to him, then reached out to take the flashlight. His hand was empty. "What the hell?" I tried again, but there was nothing for me to take. I sank back onto the bed. "Holy shit."

Vittorio went to turn the nice, safe, electric light on, and the glowing orb disappeared. "Simply put, my power is responding to yours."

"I don't have any power, whatever you mean by that." My mind raced as I tried to absorb this revelation.

"That is where you are wrong. I have never met anyone with power like yours, which I believe is why you react to me as you do. And the fact that you do not even know you have it magnifies the effect because you do not know how to control it, or even that you should control it."

"Then why aren't you affected by me as I am by you?"

"Elena, you have no idea how strongly I am affected by you, but I am familiar with my power. I have had nearly thirty years to learn to control it. Even so, you present the greatest challenge to my control I have encountered in a long time."

I thought back to the night of our first meeting, and recalled a bead of sweat trail his neck as he oh-so-properly kissed the back of my hand. At the time I dismissed it as an effect of the heat from the overhead lights, but now thought different. What about when we were bird watching? It was a pleasant day, but not too warm. Had he been sweating then, too? And tonight at the club? "If all this is true, I don't think it's safe for me to be with you. I can hardly control myself. Even now I want to pull you onto this bed with me." Panic rose in my chest. Magic? I couldn't deny what I saw. It was as good an explanation as any for my reaction to Vittorio. "Please, can Sarah take me home? I don't think I should see you anymore." I was surprised by the disappointment I heard in my voice. I was going to have to let Ms. Carmen down. This was way more than I could handle.

"There is another option." Vittorio's face was carefully neutral, but his eyes showed hope.

"What's that?" My mind screamed at me to get out, to run as far away as I could, but my legs wouldn't listen.

"I can teach you to control your power. I can help you become familiar with it. I will not lie and say that if you learn that you will no longer be affected by me, but you will be able to control your power's reaction to mine."

"What is this power?"

"I told you. Magic." He leaned forward just a little in the chair.

"But what does it do? If all it does is make people lust after each other, what's the point?"

Vittorio chuckled warmly. "Elena, it is so much more than that. That is simply the way our powers have chosen to acknowledge one another. For example, my power responds to

Samuel's combatively."

"What would you have done to him had he not apologized to me tonight? I've never seen such fear in someone's eyes."

"I honestly do not know. I am not fond of violence, but you cannot begin to understand what you mean to me. I will protect you at any cost."

"That's what I don't understand. How can I be so important to you? You don't even know me."

"I will explain it to you in time, Elena, but please be patient. There is much I must tell you, and I do not want to overwhelm you." Vittorio leaned forward, as if he wanted to reach for me, then stopped.

"Being so damned mysterious is not likely to win my trust. It's bad enough I'm affected so strongly by you, and now you tell me it's because of magic? If that really is true, how am I supposed to believe you're not using these magical powers to make me lust after you? How can I trust you?"

I forgot all about the case. Only my emotions were present. Anger, fear, confusion, and lust threatened to overwhelm me. My father had betrayed me, and he betrayed my mother when she was still alive. I did not trust men easily, and Vittorio was making it even more difficult. This night opened more emotional wounds than I cared to face.

"Elena, please tell me what you want of me. What will make me believe you?" He stood, and took a few steps toward the bed.

I wanted to shrink further away from him, but held my ground. "You can start by explaining some of this crap."

"Where do you want me to begin?"

"Tell me why I'm so damned important to you?"

"I did not fully understand it myself until tonight, but I felt drawn to you, as if there was a purpose for us meeting."

There was a purpose, alright, I thought. And it sure as hell didn't involve magic. I couldn't tell him that, though. I may have let myself get emotionally involved, but I wasn't stupid enough to tell him about the case. Not yet.

He continued. "I know now that it is our powers calling to each other, and I sense there is a deeper purpose than a romantic relationship to us being together. Also, in the interest of honesty, and at the risk of scaring you away for good, I am a hopeless romantic. I believe in love at first sight."

So much for my theory that only giggly girls fell for that. I was not a hopeless romantic, and simply didn't understand what Vittorio claimed to be feeling. I was also too tired to pursue it any further that night. "I don't get it. I don't believe in love at first sight, but for now, I'll take you at your word. Tell me more about this magic."

"It is simply that. Magic." He spread his arms, palms up, as if to illustrate how simple the concept was.

"Like in movies?"

"Kind of, yes. It is easier to explain in teaching than in words. If you become familiar with it, learn to control it, befriend it, you will be amazed at what you can do."

"Like make balls of light in my hand?"

"That is one minor thing, yes. Will you let me teach you?" He took another step toward the bed, and me.

I took a moment to consider. Magic, power, lust; could I handle it?

"Please, Elena. I do not want to lose you. But if you say no, I will respect your wishes. Sarah will take you home, and I will never bother you again." Vittorio's voice cracked with emotion.

I thought Vittorio's heart would break if I said no. Perhaps mine would, too. I walked to him, standing just inches away. "Yes." I reached up and touched his face with one hand. "Please teach me." I stood on tiptoe, rested my hands on his shoulders to steady myself, and kissed him. I nearly fell, but he caught me and held me in his arms, holding my body firmly against his while we kissed. I felt boneless. It might have been seconds or years before I stopped. "I want this."

Vittorio gently laid me down on the bed. "I gave you my word I would do no more than kiss you tonight. I am not sure I can fight this. I must leave you here to sleep, Elena."

I wanted to beg him to stay, but only nodded. He turned to walk away, and I felt a wild beast tearing its way through my body.

CHAPTER FOURTEEN

"No!" I cried out.

Vittorio turned. "What is it?"

My whole body ached. Some amorphous thing tried to tear its way out of my body. "Please, don't go," I whispered in a weak voice, clinging to the bed.

"I am sorry, Elena, I must." He turned again.

As he took a step, that thing tore out of me and rushed for him. It hurt so badly, I was surprised it had no form.

He stopped, and then collapsed to the floor. "Sarah!" he shouted.

She appeared in the doorway a moment later.

"Call Samuel. Tell him to get over here now."

The whites of Sarah's eyes showed as she wrung her hands.

"Now!" he bellowed.

She ran off, presumably to call Samuel. He was the last person I wanted to see just then. Whatever it was that was reaching for Vittorio agreed, and subsided just a little.

"I apologize, Elena, but he is the only one who can help us right now." Sweat poured down his face. He gripped the door frame in what I assumed was an attempt to keep himself from coming closer to me.

"What's going on?" Tears streamed down my face. My whole body shook.

"Your power seems to be reacting a little more strongly than I expected. It does not want me to leave. Do you feel as if something is tearing out of you?"

I nodded.

"That is your power. It is trying to bring us together."

My power flared again, reaching for him, an invisible hand pulling him toward me. I realized I was physically reaching for him. My body ached for him.

Vittorio walked to the bed, moaned wordlessly, and fell to the ground. "I do not want to hurt you. My power is responding too strongly to you. I cannot control it. I want you too badly, Elena, and while you may feel as if you want me as well, I am almost certain you will regret it once your power has subsided. Samuel must help us. I only hope I can hold out until he gets here."

"How long will that take?"

"He lives twenty minutes away. I hope he is home."

I sobbed wordlessly.

"Go into the bathroom. Lock the door."

I stood, but found myself walking toward Vittorio, not the bathroom. I closed the distance between us and wrapped my arms around him. His body burned beneath my hands, hotter than any human should be. I pulled his face down to mine, kissing him passionately.

He held my face in his hands and returned the kiss. My hands explored his body, the hard muscle beneath his clothes. I pressed myself against him even more firmly, gasped when I felt how much he wanted me. I wanted him naked with me in that bed.

"Vittorio?" Sarah had returned.

Vittorio forced his face from mine and turned to look at Sarah. "Pull Elena into the bathroom. Quickly, please."

I grasped him more tightly, against my will.

He pried my hands off him and Sarah pulled me toward the bathroom. "It hurts!" she cried out.

My power tried to push her away, violently fighting the person keeping it from what it wanted - Vittorio.

"Please Sarah, we need your help. I promise you will not be harmed, even if it hurts now. It is all in your mind; it is not real,"

Vittorio said.

She continued to drag me to the bathroom. I fought her the entire way. She pushed me in, hard, and slammed the door.

I huddled in the farthest corner on the cold tile floor, hugging my knees to my chest, crying and trying to fight the invisible thing although I didn't know how. Desperate need for Vittorio threatened my sanity. I hoped Samuel would get there soon.

Ages later, the bathroom door burst open. I thought it was Vittorio and flung myself at him, wrapping my arms and legs around his body. I was chagrined to find it was Samuel to whom I clung. My power immediately receded, disappointed.

He carried me to the bed, where I collapsed, exhausted.

I was relieved and disappointed not to see Vittorio in the room.

I resented the fact that Samuel seemed to be all I had for help. He already thought poorly of me; I didn't want him to see me so weak, so out of control. I didn't want anyone to see me like that. "What's happening to me?" He held me and stroked my hair like a child.

"Didn't Vittorio explain it to you?"

"He did, but I've never experienced magic, never knew it was real. I don't really understand what's going on. I mean, I've seen movies and stuff, but this is real. Samuel, it's real. It's happening to me. I don't understand." I hated the fact that he held me while I cried and pulled away.

"I'm sorry I'm the one here."

Was he sorry for me, or sorry for himself that he had to help Vittorio's "latest arm candy?"

"I did not understand what you were, but now I understand what Vittorio sees in you."

Was that his way of apologizing again for the way he treated me earlier? It didn't matter. "Just help me, please."

"I will do everything I can. You have my word."

I didn't believe his word was as good as Vittorio's, but I had little choice other than to accept it.

"You can sleep here tonight. Vittorio is going to stay at my house," Samuel said.

"Is that necessary?" I wanted comfort. I was in no state to be alone with my newfound power, and the next best thing to my own bed was Vittorio lying next to me.

"We're not sure, but don't want to take any chances. I will stay here tonight. In the morning, I will begin training you. If you want to be with Vittorio, we can't waste any time."

"Thank you, Samuel."

He stood.

"Will you sit with me until I fall asleep?"

He sat back down on the edge of the bed as I pulled the blanket up to my chin.

"I feel so silly. I feel like a child hiding from the monster under the bed."

"Don't feel silly, Elena. This is a dangerous thing you're dealing with. I was scared too when I discovered my power. Vittorio won't let anything happen to you though."

How the hell could I work this case when I had some crazy, magical ability I knew nothing about? How could I be objective enough when my whole body ached for this man I barely knew? I needed to get this situation - and my life - back under control as soon as I possibly could.

CHAPTER FIFTEEN

It was after noon when I woke the next day. Feeling hung-over, I stumbled to the bathroom, and checked my body for cuts and bruises. I knew nothing had physically harmed me last night, but I hurt so badly I had to check. I was injury free, except for bruises on my arms from Sarah dragging me into the bathroom.

I turned on the shower, and stood under the hot water. I didn't allow myself to cry; I'd done enough of that the night before. Crying was no way to get my life back under control. While I washed, I examined my emotions as objectively as possible.

With Vittorio nowhere near, I felt very little lust for him. It was there, just under the surface, but it was manageable. Did my feelings go deeper than mere lust? I hoped not, but feared otherwise.

Thinking of Vittorio's obvious concern for me, his tenderness, the rapture on his face during our bird watching outing made me smile. I had to be honest with myself. I was falling for him, but how much of that was because bird my power?

I hoped once I learned to control this power - whatever it was - I'd be able to better discern which of my feelings were real, and which influenced by magic.

I shivered at the thought of that word. *Magic.* Seems my mind wasn't as open as I thought it was.

I managed to find the kitchen, and was pleased to see breakfast waiting for me. My stomach growled at the scent of bacon.

"I heard the shower, so asked Sarah to fix some food for you,"

Samuel explained.

"Thanks. I'm starving." I dove into the hot scrambled eggs, crispy bacon, and warm buttery toast. "Will you tell me how you discovered your power?" I asked between mouthfuls.

"I was five years old when my power manifested," Samuel said, sipping coffee while he told me his story. "Some kids at the playground were making fun of me. One of them pushed me down. I became angry and pushed him in return, only I didn't touch him. I pushed him from ten feet away, hard enough that he flew backwards. I was lucky enough that my mother had power as well, so she knew how to train me. I've met others who didn't have that luxury, who had to figure out what the hell was going on and how to control it all by themselves."

"Guess I'm lucky to have you and Vittorio, then," I said with my mouth full of scrambled eggs.

"Yes, though Vittorio seems to be a mixed blessing at the moment. The most important thing is going to be for you to develop mental shields. You will learn to build these shields around you, to keep your power in, and others' power out. Once you learn that, we can explore other areas of your power."

"Like making light out of nothing?"

One side of Samuel's mouth turned up into a grin. "Yes. That is minor compared to much of what we can do." He went to refill his coffee mug.

"Like what?" I held my mug out for more, as well.

"Patience, Elena. Shields first, then we'll move on."

Samuel led me to a sitting room somewhere in the depths of Vittorio's mansion. I felt lost in the huge structure. I knew it was his home, but I couldn't bring myself to call it a house.

The room looked as though it was never used. It contained a nice, but boring couch, and two equally boring arm chairs to match. A huge painting of mountains and a sunset hung on one wall. Otherwise, this was the most sterile room I had ever seen in someone's home.

"You probably guessed Vittorio doesn't use this room often. That's why I chose it."

"Why would that matter?" I asked.

"Power can be unpredictable in beginners, so if it gets out of control, Vittorio will not care if anything in this room is destroyed." Samuel shrugged to illustrate the unimportance of the objects.

"Destroyed?" What was I getting into?

"I told you I pushed the boy down without touching him. Some people can manipulate objects."

"I see." My heart raced.

"First, we need to find out if, and how, your power reacts to mine. Depending on that, we may need to enlist the help of someone else," Samuel said.

"Who?" I asked.

"I don't know yet. We'll figure that out if we reach that point. I'm going to very gently push at you with my power. Nothing nearly as intense as what you experienced last night. Let me know if you feel anything."

I stood a few feet away from him. I saw no visible signs that he was doing anything, but my body began to tingle. I felt as if he was trying to invade my soul. Where last night my power was trying to tear its way out of my body, it now felt like Samuel's was trying to tear into mine. I worried he would be able to read my worst secrets. "Stop, please."

"You feel it?" His face was neutral as he watched my reaction.

"Yes. I don't like it."

"Good. That will give you more incentive to block me out."

"But last night, Vittorio didn't feel like an invasion. It was…" I trailed off, not wanting to describe my lust to Samuel.

"I know. Everyone's power is different, and reacts differently to that of others. Your power responds to Vittorio's sexually. Mine responds to him combatively. It's always different, but the methods with which you can control it, or block it out, are the same. Now, what is the strongest barrier you can picture?"

"A huge, stone wall. Like the walls of a medieval castle."

"I want you to imagine a stone wall all around your body. This wall will block any power you do not wish to feel. It will keep yours in and away from other people, and will keep others' power away from you. Close your eyes and imagine the wall. I'm going to push at you again." He rested his hands on my shoulders for a moment, steadying me, then stepped back.

I closed my eyes and concentrated on breathing. I pictured a thick, stone wall surrounding me. As I did this, I felt something push at it, as if a strong wind blew against the wall. It worked!

I opened my eyes, surprised at my success. Immediately the wall was gone, and Samuel's power threatened to overwhelm me. My power did not like his, and pushed back at him angrily, a wave of heat emanating from my body. I tried to build the wall around me again, but could not concentrate. I tried to mentally pull my power back to me, but didn't know what I was doing, so I failed. Samuel was pushed to the ground. My power seemed happy with that, and receded into my body. I felt no more heat.

He stood up and brushed himself off. "Good. You did very well before you lost focus. What did you feel?"

I told him of the wind pushing against my invisible wall.

"Excellent! That is exactly what you should feel. You are a natural at this, Elena. I think you will be an easy student to train. But you must work on your concentration. You will not always be able to stand calmly with your eyes closed. Of course we'll start off slowly, but you will need to build your shields up to a point where the slightest thought will put them into place. Do you meditate?"

"No." I sat down to catch my breath.

"I want you to meditate at least once a day for ten minutes. More will be even better. Sit quietly with your eyes half shut - not all the way shut so you won't fall asleep. Count your breaths, and try to think of nothing. Simply focus on your breath. When thoughts arise, just bring your mind back to your breathing. That will help you build focus. Now, let's try again."

We worked this way for several hours. By the time Samuel announced we had made significant progress and were done for the day, I was exhausted. "Can Sarah take me back home?" I could have asked Samuel, but didn't want to spend more time with him than was necessary. I was grateful for his help, but did not see us becoming friends anytime soon.

"Why the rush? Is someone waiting for you?"

My power flared at Samuel's inquisitiveness, heat rushing out of my body.

I closed my eyes and tried to concentrate on my wall. "No, I'm just exhausted and would like the comfort of my own home."

"I'm sorry, Elena, I didn't mean to upset you."

Again, my power flared. I shushed him so I could concentrate. I opened my eyes a minute later, after I felt in control of my power.

"Very good! You were able to control it even under stress." He smiled.

"You did that on purpose?"

"Yes. I'm very proud of you, Elena. Vittorio will be happy to hear this."

I hadn't thought of Vittorio all day. "When can I see him?"

"I think we should wait until you have a few more training sessions, though I'm sure he'd be more than happy to hear your voice tonight. And yes, Sarah will take you home."

CHAPTER SIXTEEN

I needed a nap. Hell, even though it was only six in the evening, I could probably sleep the rest of the night. My stomach growling reminded me I hadn't eaten since I woke, and that food was more important than sleep. I was too tired to cook, and didn't feel like talking to Kevin just then, so I called for Chinese delivery. I ate, but was too tired to taste the food. I left the half-empty cartons on the table, and then collapsed into bed. I had to wake up early to meet Samuel for another lesson in power control.

Sleep had barely taken over me when I was jolted awake by my cell phone. I sat up in bed abruptly, annoyed at the call, and fumbled for my phone on the bedside table. "What?"

"Elena?"

"Vittorio!" His voice caressed my body, even through the phone. I sighed happily, and settled back against the pillows.

"How are you? I have been worried."

"Exhausted. I was just falling asleep."

"Forgive me. I do not mean to rob you of your rest. I will call you tomorrow."

"No, it's alright. Please don't hang up." My exhaustion erased any chance of me pretending to be calm and collected.

"Samuel said you did well today. I am very pleased to hear that. Already, I miss you terribly."

"I miss you too," I found myself admitting. I hadn't even known it was true until the words escaped my mouth.

"I hope to see you again soon, but do not want to risk a replay of last night."

"Yeah, me too. That was scary." After a moment of silence, I asked, "Vittorio, when did you discover your power?"

"I was five years old."

"How did it happen for you?"

He was silent.

"Vittorio?" How I loved saying his name.

"I am here. It is a hard story. I would prefer to tell you in person. I do not like the phone for serious conversations. Can you wait to hear it?"

"I guess so." I didn't want to, but if that's what he wanted, I would respect that. "What did you do today? Why aren't you at The Chapel tonight?"

"I did not have the heart to go without you by my side. And I, too, am tired from the day's activities. I spent the day with my teacher for more training. It was a humbling experience. It has been a long time since anyone has been able to break through my defenses."

"I'm sorry."

"Do not be sorry, Elena. I had grown complacent. It is a good thing, in a way, this happened. It is not safe to let oneself become too secure in one's abilities. Sadly, I had done so. Perhaps had I not, last night would have been less difficult for us."

"Who is your teacher?" I realized I wanted to know everything about this man.

"A close friend of mine."

"Will you tell me about him?" I asked, and then yawned into the phone before I could stifle it.

"I will, but now I should let you sleep, mia bella. You need your rest. You will not be far from my thoughts until I can see you again."

"What does that mean? Mia whatever?"

"My beauty."

I smiled at that. "Good night, Vittorio."

"Good night, Elena. Ti amo." He hung up before I could ask

what that meant, though I had an idea. How could he love me? He barely even knew me.

Guilt washed over me. Vittorio seemed like a good person. I hated lying to him, but if my suspicions about the Elizabeth whom Samuel had taken to the premiere were right, then Vittorio could help me find Courtney. And now that I knew about magic, I understood my instinct that no one at The Chapel would readily tell me if they knew Courtney. Did she have power? Is that what Ms. Carmen meant by getting into something worse than drugs? Did she know about magic?

So many questions, and not a single answer.

CHAPTER SEVENTEEN

The next two days consisted of more grueling training with Samuel, this time at his house, which was no less grand than Vittorio's. Where Vittorio's mansion looked like a miniature medieval fortress, Samuel's was very modern, all clean lines and simple, yet elegant, decorations. It was almost sterile, as if he had designed the house for *Zen Millionaires Today*, then never gotten around to adding a personal touch after the photo shoot. I looked for photographs, but found none. I had hoped to find at least one of him and Elizabeth to confirm my suspicions, but had no such luck. There weren't any collections on display, nothing to match Ms. Carmen's story about his interest in Caribbean art or history.

In fact, there was almost no personal touch to this house. If there was, it was hidden from public view. Samuel was careful to keep me away from certain areas of his house, and that alone made me suspicious. I only found one area that showed any hint an actual human being instead of a sterile robot lived here, and part of me wished I hadn't.

After taking a wrong turn to a bathroom, I found myself in a small room, not much bigger than a walk in closet. The room held a shrine. That's all I could call it. A small table, like an altar, held photos of a beautiful young woman, though they were older. It looked like they were from the 70s and 80s. The woman held a small boy in some of them, and as they progressed I could tell the boy was Samuel. They stopped when he looked to be about ten years old. An urn sat in the middle of the table.

"You seem to have taken a wrong turn." Samuel's voice behind me startled me.

"I'm sorry, I didn't mean to..."

"My mother. She died when I was ten." He paused, lost in a memory. "Come, I'll show you the way again." He grabbed my arm a bit roughly, obviously angry at my intrusion, and led me to the bathroom.

When I returned - I was very careful not to make any wrong turns this time - Samuel had composed himself and acted as if nothing had happened. Strange. I didn't like talking about my mother, but I didn't have a shrine or act as Samuel had.

Unfortunately, practice to envision the wall to protect myself, and to keep my own power under control left me little time for any other snooping. I made mental notes of areas to investigate further if I ever go the chance, but that was about it.

When I arrived at Samuel's the fourth morning, he seemed tense. He clenched his jaw, and nervous energy radiated from him. "What's wrong? Is Vittorio okay?" My pulse quickened at the thought something might have happened to him.

"He's fine. In fact, he's on his way over here now."

"He is?" Exuberance and apprehension battled within me. I was excited to see him, but did not want a replay of the other night.

"Yes, I think you're strong enough in your control to see him. But we're going to try it here, with me present, in case I'm wrong. I need you to remain calm. You absolutely must keep your focus."

"Thank you, Samuel." My dislike for him had lessened, but hadn't dissipated entirely. If we had been better friends, I would have hugged him.

"Save that for later if this doesn't go horribly awry." It seemed as if the dislike was still mutual.

We sat in Samuel's living room. I closed my eyes and meditated, proud of myself for remaining calm. I opened my eyes when I felt Vittorio's warm energy fill the room. I jumped from the couch and ran to him, but Samuel stepped between us, stopping me from leaping into Vittorio's arms.

"Elena, remember what I said about remaining calm?" Samuel said.

"Oh. Right. Sorry." I looked down sheepishly. I wanted to make Vittorio proud; I was off to a horrible start.

"Do not be sorry. I would love nothing more than to sweep you into my arms. I understand how you are feeling," Vittorio said.

"What now?" I asked Samuel.

"Try holding hands. I think that would be the safest way to start."

"You think?" I wanted him to know beyond a doubt it was the best way to start.

"I can't be certain of anything. Magic is not always predictable, especially in those who are just learning to control it. We have to start somewhere, though."

"Okay." I took a deep breath, closed my eyes, and concentrated. Even though I had done well with my concentration and focus, I wanted as much control as I could muster before touching Vittorio. I reached out and held my hand in the air, waiting for him to take hold of it. When he did I drew a sharp breath. My body tingled, but that was all. I opened my eyes, keeping my hand in his.

"Good," Samuel said. "A very good start, Elena. Now, take his other hand."

I did, and the tingled intensified, like an electrical current that had gone full circle, but nothing bad happened. I remained in control of my power.

"Very good." Samuel looked at Vittorio, asking him a silent question. Vittorio nodded.

"Elena, I would like to try to embrace you. Do you feel strong enough for that?" Vittorio asked me.

The thought of feeling his body pressed against mine made my heart race. I closed my eyes and tried to calm my breathing. "I think so."

"I want you to be certain. If you are not, we should not

attempt this."

I wanted nothing more than to hold him, but I thought hard about whether I could maintain control. "Yes. I can do this." I kept my eyes open. Vittorio moved slowly toward me, each step causing the tingle in my body to intensify. I kept my breathing slow and even, picturing the stone wall around me. The wall seemed so real I wondered how Vittorio would step through it to hold me. Of course it didn't work that way.

He closed the distance and tentatively wrapped his arms around me. He was within the wall, yet still the wall held his power out.

My heart raced, and I felt my power come alive within my body. He held me gently, and even though I wanted to wrap myself around him as tightly as I could, I resisted the urge. I concentrated on the power in me, holding it in check. When I felt strong enough, I wrapped my arms around Vittorio, lightly at first, then lost my self control.

I held him tight, and rested my cheek against his chest. Vittorio stood still, allowing me to take the lead. The power rose in my body, but this time it did not feel as if a wild thing was trying to tear out of me. It felt like a great, warm wave, washing from side to side within me. The air around us filled with energy as Vittorio's power responded to mine.

An instant later, Vittorio's power was gone, his shields firmly in place, but mine was still alive, hot in my body. We held each other for a few minutes, and when it was clear I was able to keep my power under control, Vittorio gently let his go again. I felt my power leave my body, a slow warmth rising from me. I looked at Vittorio, alarmed.

"It is all right, Elena. Hold onto it, yet let it go at the same time. Do you understand?"

My brain didn't understand, but something deep within me did, so I nodded. I stared into his eyes as I let my power go to his. Our powers swam around us, electrifying the room. I could see them merge, his a green like the shade of a peridot crystal, mine a warm amber. Our powers met and became one, and I felt as if I could see into his soul, and he into mine. It did not feel like an invasion as when Samuel had pushed at me with his power. I kissed Vittorio passionately. The world around me disappeared; there was only the two of us, surrounded by green and orange energy.

I don't know how long we kissed. When we parted, I fell to the couch.

Vittorio sat more ceremoniously, but he didn't look much stronger than I felt. I didn't feel bad. I felt alive, exhilarated, but exhausted. I looked at him as if I were seeing him for the first time. "Wow."

"Yes, mia bella. Wow."

I laughed. Then I looked at Samuel, who had also collapsed onto a chair. "Samuel? Are you okay?"

"Yes," he said weakly. "Your powers merged together is a force to be reckoned with. I was not expecting that, and am quite drained. When one is confronted with such strong power as Vittorio's - and it seems, yours - especially combined, one must be prepared. I was not, so it took more effort for me to control my power, to prevent it from rushing to join yours. It also took more effort to keep your powers out of my psychic field."

"I'm sorry."

"Don't be. It was an amazing experience."

I looked down, heat rushing through my face. I knew what it felt like for me. I didn't want Samuel to be part of that.

"Don't be ashamed, Elena. I don't think I experienced what you and Vittorio did. I simply felt a rush of great power, but it was no more than power. There was no sex in it for me. I only mean it isn't often that one is confronted with such a force." Samuel studied us as if he had never seen us before. A hint of distrust and jealousy gleamed coldly in his eyes.

Vittorio reached for me and cupped my face in his hand, distracting me from what I saw in Samuel's eyes. I was relieved to feel nothing but a tingle. "I am so proud of you, Elena."

"Is it going to be like this every time we kiss?"

"It will not. This is the first time our powers have truly been introduced to each other. It is always the most intense the first time. We will have to practice controlling our powers together, however. It will take concentration to not experience this every time."

"Practice, huh?" I grinned at him.

He smiled. "Yes."

"No offense, Samuel, but will you have to be here when we, um, practice? It's just that this is kind of personal, and I'm not really the show and tell type," I said.

"From what I saw just now, I do not think so. Your control is strong. But in the beginning, I think it would be best if I was close by. Not in the same room, but close enough that if it gets out of control I will hear you call out and be able to come help."

"Can you accept that, Elena?" Vittorio asked.

"Do I really have a choice?" He didn't say no, but I could tell that was the answer. "Yes, I can handle that. I just prefer not to be in the same room. I'm a private person."

"I understand," Samuel and Vittorio said in unison.

I wondered if they could read each other's minds, but was too exhausted to give it much thought.

CHAPTER EIGHTEEN

I took a long nap at Samuel's before going home. I wanted nothing more than to curl up next to Vittorio and feel him hold me while we slept, but Samuel wouldn't allow it, saying I was too exhausted. He had a point.

After resting, I went home. I hadn't checked the voice mail on my cell phone for a few days, and discovered several messages from Ms. Carmen asking about my progress. The messages grew more frantic as she worried about why I didn't return her calls.

She answered on the first ring. "Elena, what's going on? Is Courtney alright?"

"I'm sorry, Ms. Carmen, I've been very sick the past few days. I'm just now starting to feel better. That's why I haven't answered the phone."

"Oh, I was worried something had happened to you."

"Like what?" I paced the kitchen.

"I don't know. I told you I don't know anything about Courtney's new friends, but I don't trust them. I don't like what my baby has become."

I was too tired to accept her continued scorn of the Gothic lifestyle. "Ms. Carmen, Goths are not dangerous. No more than any human being. Just because we choose to dress in black clothing and wear heavy makeup does not mean we are serial killers out to corrupt the youth of America. I'm sure Courtney is safe."

Silence emanated from the other end of the line. "I - I'm sorry, I didn't mean to insult you."

"I'm sure you didn't, but I'm beginning to understand why

your daughter may have wanted to run away." I wished the last part hadn't slipped out. Blaming the parent for a runaway child was never a wise move, but I was still trying to come to terms with recent events, and my filter was not up to speed.

Her voice broke. "I've been a horrible mother, haven't I?" she sniffled.

"Ms. Carmen, I'm sorry I said that. I told you I've been sick, and I'm still exhausted from that. Mothers and their teenage daughters rarely get along. I'm sure you've been a great mother, even if Courtney doesn't agree right now."

"I'm just so worried about her."

"I know. As soon as I'm better, I'll do all I can to find her. I think this Elizabeth Hardgrave may be a clue. I'm going to try to find her. Your daughter will be fine."

"Thank you, Elena." She hung up, her sobs making me feel about two inches tall.

That night, Kevin burst through the door. "Where have you been? I've been worried sick about you. Why haven't you answered your phone?"

"It's been a long, difficult couple of days. Just chill out a minute and I'll try to explain." I sat on the chair across from Kevin with my tea, and told him everything. With many interruptions, it took over an hour to try to explain it all. When I finished relating my tale of the fantastic to him, he sat with his jaw gaping, a look of disbelief on his face. "So are you going to have me committed?"

"I don't even think the psych ward would take you."

"You don't believe me."

"Give me a break, Elena. This isn't exactly the easiest thing to swallow. I'm trying, but put yourself in my shoes."

"I know it sounds unbelievable. Watch this, Kevin." I turned off the lights, closed my eyes, and concentrated. I felt the power manifest in the palm of my hand. When I opened my eyes, the room glowed with light, bright enough to show the shock on

Kevin's face. "So?" He simply stared at me with his mouth open. "What do you think?"

"Wow."

"I told you I'm not a nut job."

"Now I think you are more than ever."

I made a motion of throwing a ball, as if I would pitch the orb of light at him. He dove to the floor, and I laughed at him. "I can't hurt you with it. Once I stop concentrating on it, it disappears," I said in the darkness. I turned the lights back on.

"You should warn someone before you do that." He sat back down in the chair, visibly shaken.

"You should stop calling me a nut job. Who knows what I'll learn tomorrow."

He looked at me with a slightly frightened look on his face.

"I'm just teasing you, Kevin. Do you really think I'd do something to hurt you? You're my only friend. I'd just appreciate it if you'd be a little nicer to me right now. It's not like all this is easy for me."

"Sorry, this is quite a shock."

CHAPTER NINETEEN

Over the next couple days, Vittorio and I practiced controlling our power together. I must admit, it was a lot of fun, but it was also exhausting. By the end of the third day, Samuel declared us strong enough to be left on our own. I think what he meant was Vittorio was strong enough to control the situation if I lost control. Either way, I was relieved he wouldn't be hovering in the next room anymore.

"Does this mean I can fall asleep next to you now?"

"Yes, mia bella."

My heart leapt with joy and I hugged him.

Vittorio swept me up into his arms and carried me into his bedroom. Rich brown carpet met deep burgundy walls. A thick, velvet, chocolate brown comforter and fluffy scarlet and deep brown pillows covered the king-sized cherry wood bed. The room was elegant and beautiful.

Vittorio laid me gently on the bed, and then lay next to me. I wrapped myself around him and rested my head on his chest, surprised to discover I wanted nothing more than to be close to him. I told him as much.

"That is a good sign. It shows me you truly are gaining control of your power."

"You're not a little disappointed?" I teased. He seemed to struggle with his answer. "Come on, Vittorio. You can tell me if you are. I won't be offended."

"Perhaps a little." He grinned and kissed my forehead. "But I want to wait until you have full control. I want everything to be perfect."

I sighed, content to feel the warmth of his body next to mine. He was too good to be true. "Vittorio?"

"Yes?"

"Will you tell me about your power now?"

"I did promise, did I not?" he mused. "Yes, I will tell you now, though I warn you, it is a hard story to tell, and to hear." He sat up in bed, leaning against the headboard.

"I want to know everything about you, Vittorio." I sat up as well.

"And so you shall." He paused, gathering his thoughts. "I was five years old. My family's dog was old, sick, and in pain. We lived in the Italian countryside, and my father did not believe in spending money on pets. Rather than take him to a veterinarian to humanely euthanize him, my father took him into the backyard and shot him." I gasped. "I watched from the kitchen window. I did not understand the dog was sick and in pain. I only understood that my father had killed my best friend. I was as angry as a five-year-old can be, and my power tore out of me and through the kitchen. It looked like a tornado had hit. When my father came inside, he thought I had thrown everything around. He beat me, and sent me to my room for the rest of the day with no food.

"The next day he told me apologize to my mother for making such a mess. I refused, and yelled at him for killing my dog. He slapped me, and again my power tore through the room. This time, my parents saw what happened, but did not understand. My mother took me to a string of doctors, but no one could explain what was going on with me. Over the years, my episodes, as my mother liked to call them, got worse. She did not know what to do with me, and eventually checked me into a mental hospital."

"Oh my god, that's horrible!" My hand went to my mouth.

"It turned out to be the best thing she could have done for me. The doctors there did not know any more than the others had, and eventually they kept me on sedatives so I could do no damage to anything or anyone."

"Anyone?"

"Yes." A pained look crossed his face. "I had an incident with one of the nurses. The first time they tried to inject sedatives in me, when I was ten, my anger took over. I threw her across the room with my power, and her head smashed against the wall. She lived, but her brain was severely damaged, and she could not function on her own." He looked away from me, as if afraid I would be disgusted with him.

I reached out and touched his face. "It's okay, Vittorio. You couldn't help yourself."

He looked at me.

"I can't think of anything you could tell me that would make me turn away from you."

Relief flooded his face, and a small smile graced his lips. He continued. "They kept me on sedatives for several months. I do not really know how long. One of the doctors, Julian Fondazione, had power and heard about me. He convinced the hospital to let him take over my case, and stopped the sedatives. He worked with me, taught me control. Eventually, I was declared safe to be released to society. My parents, however, wanted nothing to do with me, so Julian took me in and continued my training. He also trained me in witchcraft."

"Witchcraft?"

"Yes. If you like, I can teach you as well. It complements our power nicely."

"I think I'd like that." Anything that would help me control this power was a positive. As well as anything to help me with the case, I grudgingly admitted to myself.

"As you wish." He kissed me lightly, and then continued his story. "When I was twenty, Julian moved here to America, and I came with him. I had nowhere else to go, and no plans. I had just graduated university, and had no idea what I wanted to do with my life, so I moved here. I got a job at Porter Enterprises, the company Samuel's father owns. That's how I met Samuel. I moved up in the company quickly, in part because of my friendship with Samuel, but mostly because I worked hard. I am now Vice President of Human Resources. Samuel is Vice President of Marketing. Our business views sometimes clash, but we manage to remain good friends most of the time."

I wrapped my arms around him, regretting for him that he had such a difficult time in the beginning. I said nothing, sensing that he knew my thoughts.

"Thank you for understanding, Elena."

"Thank you for telling me." I stared into his eyes, and then kissed him. My power remained calm this time, but the kiss was still incredible.

I fell asleep with Vittorio holding me, and had the best night of sleep I'd had since this whole thing began.

CHAPTER TWENTY

The next afternoon, Vittorio called me to ask if I would join him at The Chapel that night.

"Of course!" I wanted nothing more than to see him again. It had only been hours since I left his house, but I missed him already.

"May I pick you up?"

"Of course. I'll warn you, though; Kevin will probably want to meet you. He's been hounding me about you since we met." Silence. "Vittorio? You're not jealous of Kevin, are you?" I'd told Vittorio about our close friendship, trying to make it as clear as possible it was strictly platonic.

"No, it is not that." He paused. "How much have you told him?"

"Everything."

"Everything?"

"Yes. I told you; he's my best friend, and like a brother to me. He stuck by me through some really hard times. We don't keep any secrets from each other."

"You trust him?"

"Completely. Please don't be mad I told him."

"I am not upset, Elena, but you must realize how unbelievable our power can be to those who do not possess it. I am not the only person I know who has been committed by family or friends because of it. It would devastate me if anything happened to you."

"You can trust Kevin. He's always taken care of me, or at least tried when I wouldn't let him." I realized it should be my turn to

79

tell Vittorio about my past. It was only fair, but I didn't want to think about that just yet. Right now, I was more concerned about Vittorio being upset I had told Kevin. I desperately wanted them to like each other. "Please, Vittorio. Kevin's all I have."

"All?" The pain in his voice was almost tangible.

"Well, he was until I met you." An image of him smiling appeared in my head. That was weird. It was so vivid, as if it had appeared on a movie screen.

"I cannot be upset about anything that is so important to you, mia bella. Of course I will meet him tonight. Shall I pick you up at nine?"

After I hung up, I went next door to Kevin's to find him watching an old UFC fight on TV. "Hey, Kev. Guess what?" I sat next to him on the couch.

"You're dropping the case?"

"No. Tonight's your big night. Vittorio's coming to pick me up at nine, so you'll get to meet him."

"About time I get to check this guy out." He turned down the volume on the TV.

"Kevin, this may be a job for me, but I really like him."

"I know that."

"I'm falling in love with him, Kevin. Please behave. Don't embarrass me."

"Would I do that?" he asked with an air of amusement giving away his best innocent face.

I glared in response.

"I'll be on my best behavior. Should I wear a suit and tie?"

I groaned in exasperation.

I tidied up my place a little before showering. I looked at the trashcans in the living room under the leaky pipes. I knew my duplex wasn't the nicest place ever, but that was downright embarrassing. Kevin could easily move someplace else. He made good money at his job repairing cars. He just didn't care, and figured it was easier to stay than go through the hassle of moving.

I, on the other hand, had no choice. Cases were sporadic. Some months I barely made rent. I didn't like how desperately I needed the money from Ms. Carmen's case, but it was true.

I decided that after I showered, I'd put the trashcans out on the back porch for the evening. Insecure - who, me? I still wasn't quite sure what Vittorio saw in me. He had everything, while I had nothing. I sighed, and then went upstairs to get ready.

CHAPTER TWENTY-ONE

It felt like bringing a boyfriend home to meet my parents for the first time, with Kevin sitting on the couch waiting for Vittorio to arrive. When we heard his car outside, Kevin jumped up to peek out the window. "Damn! Nice car! How the hell does that guy afford a Ferrari?"

I simply shrugged. I knew he afforded it easily, but was too nervous to form a coherent sentence.

I opened the door before Vittorio reached it, but restrained myself enough to stand and wait for him, rather than run into his arms. I still wasn't entirely comfortable with being so completely enamored of a man.

Vittorio came to me and initiated the kiss.

Even in four-inch heels, I had to stand on tiptoe to kiss him. It should have been a quick kiss, but my power had other ideas. I kept it under control, mostly, but it rose in my body to meet Vittorio's. We kissed passionately. "Wow," I breathed when we pulled apart. "I'm still amazed by that."

"Holy shit," Kevin said from the couch. "What the hell was that?"

Our power must have enveloped Kevin, sending shockwaves through his body.

Vittorio chuckled, low and warm, and said, "Perhaps it is a good thing you told him."

Kevin looked a bit frightened, and I couldn't blame him. At least he had a little warning, unlike my first cruel experience. "I've got beer in the fridge for you Kevin."

"Yeah, I think I'll get one." He went into the kitchen, and I heard him pop open a can.

"Will he be alright?" Vittorio asked.

"Yeah, he'll get over it."

A few minutes later, having chugged his beer, Kevin returned. "Sorry, I just wasn't expecting that."

"I'm sorry, Kevin. Apparently I don't quite have complete control yet." I cleared my throat as heat rose in my cheeks, then introduced them.

Vittorio held out his hand to shake Kevin's. After a moment of hesitation, Kevin shook his hand. He sighed in relief when nothing happened. "Nice ride."

"Thank you."

"You're going to take care of Elena, right? Because power or no power, you'll have to answer to me if anything happens to her."

"I will take the utmost care of her." He placed his right hand over his heart, as if making an oath.

"Good. Well, you two have fun. I'm going to go watch some wrestling." He left before I could say goodbye.

"Guess he's a little shocked by our display," I said. In response, Vittorio kissed me again. "Do we have to go to The Chapel?"

"I should at least put in an appearance. Rumors are bound to be flying by now. There are others who know of the power. I do not think we will be able to hide yours from them. I trust Samuel to have said nothing, but these things have a way of getting out anyway. Will you be comfortable with that?"

"Do I really have a choice? I mean, I'm not sure about it myself yet, but I've never cared much what other people think about me."

"Elena, you must understand. Before this, the women despised you because you won my affections so quickly. Of those who know, everyone will be wary of you now, men and women. New, untested power can be a dangerous thing. Some will try to woo you away from me, but they will not have your best interests in mind. They will want to use you, to mold you to their plans."

"And what are you doing? How can I know you aren't trying to mold me to your own plans?"

"Elena, please trust me. I would do nothing to harm you. Ti amo, mia bella." He held my hands.

"I love you, too, Vittorio." The words escaped my lips before I could think.

Vittorio looked at me in wonder. "Do you mean that?"

"Yes," I said without hesitation. "I love you. And I do trust you." I smiled. "It feels good to say that. But I'd like to hear you say it in English."

"I love you, Elena." He kissed me, and this time, I did not try to hold my power back. I let it go to him, surround him, pull him to me.

I didn't realize I had been pulling him towards the stairs to my bedroom when he pulled away. "Elena, we should stop."

"I don't want to."

"Neither do I, but you don't have full control yet. I don't want anything to harm you in any way."

"Would sex hurt me?"

"Not physically, but it can be extremely intense when two people with power make love. It reaches into the other's soul, and can be a very painful, emotional experience if one is not prepared for it."

"How do you know?"

"I made love with a woman who had power. It was long ago, when I was still learning. I was not ready for it, and thought she would rip my soul from my body."

I felt a tinge of jealousy, which must have showed on my face. I knew it was silly; of course he'd had sex with other women. I was no virgin either.

"Elena, please do not be jealous. It was many years ago when I still lived in Italy, and I do not even know what has become of the woman. In any case, I do not think very highly of her because of what she did to me. I do not want you to experience that."

I sighed. "Alright. But we better go, because my self-control isn't going to hold out much longer."

Vittorio chuckled and kissed me on the cheek.

CHAPTER TWENTY-TWO

This was the second time I arrived at The Chapel with Vittorio. Again, I felt like someone walking down the red carpet. However, this time, it had the feel of someone who had been away in rehab or jail, and everyone was curious about the experience. I was uncomfortable. I wanted to talk to Bryn before I had to deal with anyone else, and told Vittorio I would meet him upstairs.

He agreed, seeming to sense my unease.

"Been a while, girl. I was starting to worry about you. Have you heard any of the rumors about you?"

"No." Vittorio had said there might be rumors. How much did Bryn know?

"Well, the big one in the general population is you, Vittorio, and Samuel being lovers. The other one I've heard floating around, and this is limited to Vittorio's crowd, is that he's grooming you for some sort of ritual or something."

"A ritual?" What on earth did she mean?

Bryn nodded.

"What kind of ritual?"

"No idea. Be careful, Elena."

"I will. Thanks for the warning. But Vittorio wouldn't hurt me."

"Others might, though." She moved to the other end of the bar to serve a customer.

When I got to the balcony, Vittorio embraced me and whispered in my ear. "We need to talk, mia bella," and he led me toward the little office.

My detective brain kicked in, and I made a mental note of everything in the office, feeling guilty for it the entire time. It housed a small desk and comfortable-looking chair, with another chair to the side, presumably for visitors. A two-drawer file cabinet sat in the corner. The desk held only a pen cup; no papers. There wasn't a hint of anything out of the ordinary. I would have to look through the filing cabinet to even hope to find any useful information.

"Did Bryn tell you any of the rumors?"

"A couple. One is quite amusing."

"Others are not so amusing. Which did she tell you?"

I told him the one about him grooming me for a ritual. "Are you?"

"Absolutely not. I told you, I would do nothing to harm you. I did hear that rumor, though. I believe it has something to do with my spiritual practices."

"Witchcraft?"

He nodded. "I know many who share my beliefs, but that does not stop them from petty jealousy."

"What are they jealous of?" I sat on the visitor chair.

"My success in the business world and the strength of my power. Yes, we perform rituals. Yes, I offered to teach you about witchcraft, but I am not grooming you for anything."

"I believe you, Vittorio. Bryn told me to be careful of these people. How much do I need to worry?"

"Be aware of your surroundings, but I do not think you have much to fear, at least not here. You know this is a VIP area. It is limited to those with power, or those very close to us. Most of them are all talk. Samuel and I will try to find out if there is anything deeper to the rumors, though. My heart would break if anything happened to you, mio amore." He wrapped his arms around me, and I knew he would keep me safe. "Shall we return to our curious bystanders?"

"I want to ask you one more thing before we do. When we

were talking on the phone earlier, and I said Kevin was all I had until I met you, I saw an image of you in my head, smiling. It was so real, like you were sitting right across the table from me. Was it just my imagination?"

"No, mio amore, it was not. I have the ability to project my thoughts into people's minds, a sort of silent communication."

"Can you read my mind?" Panic filled my gut. Did he know the truth about me, about my investigation?

"I cannot. I can sense emotions, but cannot read minds. There are some who can, but it is a rare talent. They must constantly work to block out the noise. Some might envy the talent, but not I. I admit there are times when it would be useful, but it would not be worth it to me."

I nodded, attempting to hide my sigh of relief.

We left the office, Vittorio locking it behind him.

CHAPTER TWENTY-THREE

We found Samuel in the balcony area outside the office arguing with two other men and a woman I recognized as Elizabeth Hardgrave.

"I told you, you are mistaken. No one is usurping your place in the coven, least of all a newcomer. She does not even know our ways yet," Samuel said.

" 'Yet.' Even you admit she is going to learn. And then what?" Elizabeth asked.

"And then if she is strong enough, she may displace you, but it will be a long time before that is even a possibility. Why don't you stop trying to cause problems?" Samuel said, jaw clenched.

"Your friend is the one causing problems by bringing this little girl into our world. We can see what he's doing. We know he's just using her to secure his place in the coven," Elizabeth said.

"Who the hell are you calling a little girl?" I couldn't help myself. I would not stand by and let some stranger insult me.

"You, little girl." Elizabeth eyed me with hatred I didn't think possible for a person one didn't know.

"I'd watch your mouth if I were you." I clenched my fists at my sides.

"Or what? You can't even control your power. We all heard about what happened."

"Is that what you think?" I knew I was taking a risk, but it was one I was willing to take. I steadied my breathing and let my power rise up in me. I didn't know what would happen. I had only focused on controlling how it reacted to Vittorio. I didn't know how it would react to my anger towards these people. It rose, hot and liquid inside me.

Instinctively, I knew what to do. I let it slowly reach out toward the three arguing with Samuel, while picturing bolts of electricity in my mind. I only wanted to scare them, to prove I had control over my power. The thought that I might prove them right never crossed my mind.

Samuel took a few steps toward me, and I saw Vittorio shake his head out of the corner of my eye. I pictured lightning surrounding Elizabeth and those accompanying her, calling my power back to me only after they had cried out in pain. It came reluctantly, wanting to play with these people who had insulted me, but it returned, allowing me to push it down to wherever it was that it slept in my gut. I collapsed, and Vittorio caught me and helped me to the couch. The look of terror on their faces was well worth the energy spent.

"What were you saying?" I knew it lost a bit of impact as I sat on the couch, but I had proven my point.

They stayed as far away from me as they could as they made their way to the stairs.

"Do you realize you just solidified their fear that you are going to try to usurp their place?" Vittorio said angrily.

Was it anger at me, or them? Maybe both.

"They insulted me, and you. I couldn't just stand by and take it."

"You have never used your power in such a way. What if you lost control? You would have confirmed their belief that you are weak." His fists were clenched as well.

Definitely at me.

"I thought of that, but it was too late by the time I did. Luckily I kept control."

"You did very well, I must admit, mia bella, but that was a very dangerous risk to take. I would appreciate it if you do not take such risks in the future," he said, jaw clenched.

"I'm sorry. I had to do something. I'm not the type of girl who stands by helpless while she's insulted." *Not anymore, anyway*, I added in my mind.

"I understand, mio amore. And I am proud of you." His voice softened as he held me close, and my power rushed out toward him.

"Oh, shit," I had time to say before I lost control. I kissed Vittorio madly, as if my life depended on it. Some tiny bit of sanity left in my brain told me I was about to give the club an X-rated show, but my body didn't care. I straddled him on the couch, pulling his shirt over his head, kissing his neck.

He neither reciprocated nor pushed me away.

After what seemed like eternity, I felt someone embrace me from behind. Someone with strong arms pulled me close to him, away from Vittorio. I struggled for a moment, but as soon as I was no longer touching Vittorio, my power calmed. Realizing it was Samuel who held me, I relaxed in his grip and let him carry me to a chair, to sit by myself.

Focusing on my breathing, I had my power completely under control again in a few minutes. I wanted to sink into the chair and disappear when I realized everyone was staring at me. As it was, all I could do was smooth down my skirt and wonder if Courtney was among the gawkers, too weak to do more than wonder.

Samuel sat on the couch next to Vittorio. I could not hear their conversation, but their faces were serious. They stood, and Vittorio headed for the stairs.

Samuel scooped me up into his arms with strength surprising for his size. He followed Vittorio out of the club, and helped me into the passenger seat of his Range Rover. Samuel and Vittorio stood outside the door of the SUV.

"I don't think I can ever show my face in there again." I groaned.

"Do not be embarrassed, mio amore."

"Easy for you to say. You weren't the one acting like a sex-crazed animal."

"You were spent from your first display of power. You did not have enough to hold it back from me. I am thankful I was strong enough to resist returning your advance."

My body tingled, craving Vittorio's touch. I tried to get out of the SUV and go to him, but Samuel held me back.

"Samuel, do you think you can give her some of your power, so she will be able to control her own?"

"Can't I just go home and sleep?" I asked.

"We have much we must discuss, the sooner the better.," Vittorio said.

"How will Samuel give me his power?"

A crowd of gawkers had gathered around the entrance to The Chapel and were staring at us.

"Samuel will explain on the drive back to my house. I think we should leave now, though, before we attract any more attention."

I wanted to protest, wanted to ride with Vittorio, but knew why I couldn't, so simply nodded. I wanted to know more about the coven, but also wanted to go home and sleep. I wondered if I could at least convince them to let me have a hot bath and some coffee before we talked about whatever was on their minds.

CHAPTER TWENTY-FOUR

On the drive to Vittorio's house, Samuel tried to explain the process of transferring energy, but as I had found with much relating to power, it was not easy to put into words, or to understand. I decided to trust him and let him do whatever was necessary. I didn't have the strength to fight.

I was careful to avoid getting too close to Vittorio when we arrived to avoid a replay of what happened at The Chapel. Samuel pulled a chair close to face me while I sat on the couch. He held my hands. Outwardly, it seemed as if he was just sitting there, but I felt his power pulse through the room. His aura was the brown of an oak tree. A moment later, I felt it push into my body. I tried to fight it, but he told me to relax. When I stopped fighting his power, it flowed easily into my body, and I immediately felt stronger, less weary. He pulled his power back into him, and I craved more.

"It is nothing to fear," Vittorio explained when I expressed my fear of the craving. "Think of it like this; when you are hungry and have not eaten for a long time, if someone takes your plate away when you are only half finished, you still want more, do you not?"

I nodded.

"It is the same with power. Samuel shared some of his energy with you, as you were drained. Of course he can not give you all his energy, and when he pulled away you were still tired, so your power wanted more."

It made sense. I realized I was looking into Vittorio's eyes while he spoke, and I felt nothing. Well, maybe not nothing, but I no longer wanted to jump his bones.

I wanted to learn more about the coven as quickly as I could, so decided to pass on asking for a bath, but insisted on coffee. When it was brewed I held the mug in both hands for warmth, though I didn't think the chill I felt was the kind to be chased away by hot liquid or a blanket.

"We need to talk about the rumors which have stemmed from my absence at The Chapel," Vittorio began.

"Yeah, and what about me kicking people out of their place in the coven?"

"I was not trying to hide anything from you, Elena. I swear it. I would hide nothing from you."

Nothing? I wondered how true that was. "Really?"

"Elena, please believe me. It has been a very busy two weeks for us all. I have not had time to tell you everything about myself. And remember, I still know very little about you and your past." It looked as if he immediately regretted that last part. "I am sorry. I should not have said that. I do not want to push you to tell me anything you do not want to."

"It's okay, Vittorio. I understand." I reached out to cup his face in my hand to emphasize that I was not angry with him.

He leaned in to kiss me, but Samuel interrupted.

"Let's stay on track, you two. Elena, it's true. Vittorio has told me of his love for you, and I feel the truth in his words."

I, too, felt the truth in both Vittorio's and Samuel's words. That was something new about my power, if sensing truth really was an aspect of it. I would have to ask Vittorio about that later.

"Okay, fine. I believe you. But I still don't understand what's going on. Why are they so threatened by me? And just what is your position in the coven?"

"I am La Guardia, the guardian of the Sacerdote. He trains others, but I am the one he teaches the most secret rituals to in order to carry them on through the generations. Some speculate that I want to take control, but that is simply not true. I do not wish to have that responsibility. The greedy ones do not understand that. Now that you are in the picture, they think I am going to use you to solidify my power and position."

"But why me? Why would I have anything to do with that? And what's a Sacerdote?" I stumbled over the unfamiliar word.

"Sacerdote is the High Priest. Sacerdotessa is the High Priestess. It is true I have never been so easily enchanted by any woman as I have been by you, mio amore. You come from nowhere, steal my heart, then we disappear from their sight for nearly two weeks after you come into your power. Most thought your dizzy spell was from alcohol, but some saw it for what it was; our powers acknowledging each other. Those are the ones who started the rumors."

"Were the three who insulted me tonight any of them?" I didn't let on that I knew who Elizabeth was. Knowing she was against us caused me to question Samuel's loyalty. What was his relationship with her?

"Yes, they are the most vocal. And now they will be even more fearful than before."

"Why?"

"Because of the strength of your power. You should not have been able to control it as well as you did tonight after so little training. Perhaps you could have sent the power out to them, but most would have lost control at that point, and the consequences would have been unpleasant to say the least. But you gave them the slightest taste of your power, then called it back to you. Yes, you were drained afterwards, but you have no idea how powerful a display that was. If I did not know your sensitive, kind nature, I would understand their fear. But while I do not know much about you, Elena, I do know you would never use your power for ill. I know they have nothing to fear, but they do not know you as I do."

"What do I do now? How do I convince them I don't care about them? And why are they so afraid of you trying to take over?"

"I do not know the answer to your first two questions. That is what we will have to figure out. For now, I do not think there is much we can do to convince them otherwise. As for why they are afraid of me trying to take control of the coven, now is the perfect time. Our Sacerdote, Clavius, is weakened. The Sacerdotessa, Aerin, who is also his wife, was killed in a burglary of their home a few months ago. He has not recovered from losing her, so if someone is going to try to overthrow him, now is the time. Since I am La Guardia, it would be logical for me to try. They don't understand that I would never betray him. Now that you are in the picture, they believe you could easily take the place of Sacerdotessa alongside me."

"I fear a power struggle will rear its ugly head soon," Samuel said.

Vittorio sighed. "I fear you are correct. I would love nothing more than to simply step down and let them fight amongst themselves. But I have seen their character. I can not in good conscience let any of them take control of the coven. It is not a position I desire, but I desire it to be in their hands even less." When Vittorio looked at me again, the pain in his eyes nearly broke my heart. "I am so sorry, mio amore."

"For what?"

"For what you are about to experience. Because of what you mean to me, you will be caught up in the power struggle that is likely to occur."

"I don't care about any of that. I don't want any power in this coven."

"They will not believe you. If you want to walk away, I will understand. It will break my heart, but it may be the best thing for you. If you leave, and never speak to me again, I will help you find another teacher." Tears glistened in his eyes.

"No," I sobbed, surprised to find my own tears. I clung to his hands. "I won't leave. I love you. I can't leave you."

"I told you I would not let any harm come to you. I will do my best, but may not be able to keep that promise if you stay with me through this fight."

"I don't care."

"At least think about it. Please, mio amore. I do not want to see you hurt." He pulled away from me slightly.

"There's nothing to think about."

"Elena, you're tired. It's been a trying night for us all. Don't make any rash decisions one way or the other right now. Vittorio is right. You should at least think about leaving," Samuel said.

I glared at Samuel. I felt the electric power rising in my body again. How dare he tell me how to live my life? Samuel looked at me in alarm, which was enough to keep me in check. I pushed my power back down, convinced it that Samuel was not the enemy. It receded, but didn't believe me.

"Very good. Control under emotional stress. I understand why they are frightened of you," Samuel said.

I thought I saw something less than honorable flicker in his eyes, but it could have just been the tears blurring my vision. Instead, I looked at the pain in Vittorio's eyes. "I'll consider it, but I won't be happy about it. I tell you I love you, and you ask me to leave in the same night. Is Sarah here? I want to go home."

"You can stay in the guest bedroom if you like," Vittorio said.

"I'm not very happy with you right now. I'd rather not be here." I sat back on the couch, arms crossed over my chest, like a sullen teenager.

Vittorio slumped in his chair, and I wanted to apologize, to hold him, tell him I didn't mean it. But I did mean it. I felt like a fool.

"Very well. Sarah will take you home. I am sorry for any pain I have caused you, mio amore."

"I know you don't mean it." I caved in and let him embrace me before I left. The warmth of his arms almost changed my mind about going home, but I was angry with him. I had to be stronger than that.

CHAPTER TWENTY-FIVE

I sat at the kitchen table massaging my temples, a cup of coffee cooling in front of me, when Kevin burst through the door the next morning. My inner conflict and guilt was growing stronger every day. Why oh why did I have to fall in love with Vittorio?

"What's wrong?" Kevin asked when I didn't look up.

"Vittorio's coven is about to have a major power struggle, with yours truly in the center of it all." I took a sip of coffee, making a face when I found it was cold.

I went round and round with Kevin again about getting out and being careful. Eventually he gave up, knowing that when I had my mind set, nothing could change it.

"What did you think of Vittorio?" I changed the subject.

"Hard to say. I was too shocked by your little display of whatever the hell that was. I guess he seems alright." Kevin shrugged his shoulders.

"At least you didn't immediately hate him." I dumped my coffee in the sink and poured a fresh cup.

"What is it about him that you like so much?" Kevin asked for what seemed like the thousandth time.

I tried once again to explain what I still didn't quite understand myself. "He's not like any other man I've ever met. He seems honorable, which is rare in this day and age. He respects me. And he seems to truly love me."

"And he's hot. But don't you dare ever tell anyone I said that."

"You know I've never been fazed by a pretty face."

Kevin raised an eyebrow.

"Yes, he's hot, but that has nothing to do with why I like him. I feel like I can trust him."

"And yet you're lying to him about your job."

I glared at Kevin. "I'm not lying."

"You're not being completely honest, either. If he's such a great guy, if you really do love him, you should come clean before things go too far."

"I know, but I don't know how." I sat back down at my kitchen table, too weak to stand. Continuing to hide the truth about my job to Vittorio made my stomach knot.

"Just tell him," Kevin said, as if it were so simple.

"But what if he hates me for it?"

"Then you deserve it."

Kevin may as well have punched me in the stomach, but I knew he was right. He was always blunt, one of the things I loved and hated about him. "But I was trying to do my job."

"Your job wasn't falling in love. Look, Elena, you know I'm here for you, but I hate seeing you like this. And Vittorio seems to make you happy. If he is as good as you say he is, I don't want you to lose that. You really should be honest with him."

When Kevin left, I decided it was time to suck it up and call Vittorio. Of course I wasn't going to leave him. I didn't want to fight over this, but it was time to be honest, and I thought that would almost certainly lead to an argument. That's if I had luck on my side. If I didn't, well, I couldn't stand the thought of that.

Maybe I could put it off a little longer. If he did hate me for it, he might not help me find another teacher, and as much as I hated having this power, it was necessary to learn how to control it. I had no idea how to go about finding a teacher on my own. It's not as though I could find someone with power to help me in the yellow pages.

No, that was selfish. I would tell him. Kevin was right; I deserved whatever I got.

"Vittorio, can I come over and talk to you? I'd like to discuss something with you in person rather than on the phone."

"You are always welcome." I noted the careful lack of 'mio amore,' as if he were certain I was going to leave him and was already trying to put a wall around his heart.

"I'll be over soon. Bye, Vittorio."

"Goodbye, Elena." The word seemed to hold more meaning than simply ending a phone call.

When Vittorio opened the door, I wrapped my arms around him and held on for dear life.

After a few moments he pulled away. "Elena, are you alright?"

"I'm not leaving you, Vittorio. I don't want to."

"Are you certain?" His eyes widened in disbelief.

"You sound like you want me to leave." Surely he wasn't going to push me away?

"I can hardly bear the thought of losing you, but I want you to be safe."

"Safe is nice, but I'd rather be with you."

He pulled me close again and relief washed through his body and into mine. His power was tinged with apprehension.

"We'll be fine as long as we have each other," I said.

"You are absolutely sure you want to put yourself in the middle of all this?" He pulled back and held me at arm's length.

Since I couldn't wrap my arms around him, I rested my hands on his forearms. "I told you I'm not leaving you. I love you. And if you don't stop trying to push me away, you're going to make me think you don't love me in return, so why don't you shut up and kiss me?"

He did just that.

Again, I found myself trying to pull him to the bedroom, and again, he stopped me. I groaned in frustration. "Are you trying to make me lose my sanity with wanting you?"

"Elena, we have discussed this."

"I know, but you make it so hard." I pouted.

"I make it hard?" He raised an eyebrow at me, and I playfully slapped his arm.

"You know what I mean. Alright, I guess we better get down to business if we can't have any fun. What's the next step in my training?"

Vittorio led me down the hallway into his study as he spoke. "There are now two things I need to teach you, and the sooner you learn, the better. You need to continue working on controlling your power, and more specifically, not draining yourself of energy when you use it. Then, we will work on what you can do with that power.

"I also need to start teaching you the ways of witchcraft, its history, the way the coven works and how its members fit together, the rituals, holidays - "

"Slow down. That's a lot of information." My head spun from the prospect of so much information.

"It will be much to take in. First I must ask you something, and I need you to be honest with me." He pulled two chairs to face each other.

I sat. "Alright."

"Do you want to join the coven?"

Silence filled the space between us as if it were something tangible. "I don't know. I mean, I don't know anything about it, so it's kind of hard to make a good decision. Can I learn about it before answering?"

"Of course, but if you fight by my side during this power struggle, depending on the outcome, you may not have a choice."

"What do you mean?"

"I should rephrase that. You always have a choice, but if the outcome is in our favor, it is possible you will have earned a powerful position in the coven."

"What position?" Why wouldn't he tell me? What was so bad to require this hinting around?

"It all depends on the outcome. I will explain more as we get into details. Keep in mind you may have that choice to make."

"I guess you better start teaching me, then."

For several hours we worked on conserving energy when I used my power. "Imagine that you are dividing your power within you. Only send out a small part of it. If you do this, you may still be a little tired afterwards, but will have plenty of energy left to remain in control of your power. There will be times when you must use everything you have, but those are rare occasions. The majority of the time, using only a small fraction will suffice."

It took several tries for me to begin to get the hang of this technique. By the time I started to figure it out, I was pretty drained.

Vittorio called an end to training for the day.

"Can I stay here tonight? I want to fall asleep next to you again."

"Mio amore, you do not even have to ask. I told you, you are always welcome here."

CHAPTER TWENTY-SIX

"I want to tell you about my past," I said as we lay in bed that night.

"I love you for who you are. Whatever is in your past cannot change that." Vittorio kissed my forehead.

"I'm not saying it would or should, but my past is kind of ugly. I only mean I want you to know me, as I want to know you."

"Very well then, mio amore."

I sat up, propping pillows against the headboard. "There's nothing really exciting to tell before I was fourteen. I was popular in grade school and had a lot of friends. That carried over into my freshman year of high school. I guess I was kind of stuck up. I had everything I ever wanted, and I knew it. I was in drama club, and was the first freshman ever to get the lead in the fall musical. I thought my life was perfect." I stared at a speck of lint on the blanket, trying to distance myself from the pain of the memories.

"My mom was a music teacher. In November of that year, she went out of town for a seminar that would introduce new methods of teaching music. When she was driving home, she was hit by a semi whose driver had fallen asleep. She was pronounced dead at the scene. My mom was my best friend. I was devastated."

"I am so sorry, Elena."

"Oh, there's more," I said bitterly. "Turns out my father was having an affair. I don't think my mom knew. His mistress showed up at the funeral to comfort my father. I don't know if he invited her. I never bothered to ask. I didn't say a word to her, but I slapped my father across the face in front of everyone and told him

I never wanted to speak to him again. I told him he had no right to be there and demanded that he leave. That was at the funeral parlor, right in front of Mom's casket." I paused, wiping tears from my face. It had been years since I had talked to anyone except my therapist about this.

"At the cemetery, before they lowered the casket, I lost it. I threw myself onto the casket, and they had to pull me away. I watched while they lowered the casket and buried it. I just sat there on the ground, crying hysterically. When the workers finally left, I sat on the fresh earth and apologized to Mom. I told her I was sorry for causing a scene, and pleaded with her not to leave me alone in the world. I realize now how silly that was. It's not like she was going to come back to life."

"It is not silly, Elena." Vittorio cupped my face in his hand.

I gave him a weak smile. "I stayed with a friend for a few weeks. Going back to school was hard. I cried a lot. My so-called friends didn't understand. They had never endured such a tragedy. They didn't know how devastating it was, and started to drift away from me, leaving me alone at lunch to cry onto my tray. Everyone in the musical started to hate me, too. Opening night was two weeks away, and my performance was awful. They didn't have enough time for someone else to learn the part, though, so they hoped for the best.

"On opening night, I refused to come out of the dressing area. That's when it really hit me that Mom wouldn't be there for my big night. I didn't care about the show anymore. I refused to act, and they had to call the whole thing off. That may as well have been the end of my high school career. The musical was a big deal at my school. Any friends who had held on abandoned me at that point. I bounced from relative to relative, staying with each one long enough to test their sanity, and then moving on." I stopped and tried to compose myself.

"You don't have to tell me this if it is too painful," Vittorio said, gently rubbing my back.

I ignored him and continued. "I pretty much quit going to school. After a few months, I managed to befriend some of the other outsiders, the druggies. I took any kind of drug they gave me, drank, you name it. I racked up quite the juvenile record with shoplifting and dropped out of school altogether the day I turned sixteen. My relatives couldn't handle me, so I stayed with my new friends whenever I could, slept on the street when I couldn't. My father reported me as a runaway, so whenever I encountered a cop, they'd hauled me back to my father's house. I was out the door again as soon as the cop pulled away each time.

"You'd think after almost two years I would have come to terms with Mom's death, but I was in too much a haze to know what was going on. Kevin tried to make me stay with him. He's two years older than me and had just gotten his own apartment. I did for a while, but he constantly lectured me about my behavior, so I left and didn't speak to him for a long time. I probably should have died from an overdose, or sleeping in the streets in the middle of winter, or any other of a dozen reasons. Somehow, I didn't.

"When I was seventeen, I agreed to help my friends rob a convenience store. We had no idea what we were doing, and stupidly chose one in a strip mall with a police sub station. Once they realized what was going on everyone scattered. I was so drugged up I just stood there confused, and I was arrested and sent to juvie for several months. I thought I would die from the pain of withdrawal. They made me talk to a counselor, and when they finally released me it was under the condition that I continue seeing a psychiatrist and check in once a month for drug tests. The psychiatrist prescribed Zoloft to help even out my mood. That's the other reason I don't drink."

"At some point we will want to try to get you away from that. You will have even more focus and control of your power when you are unmedicated, but that can wait."

"Good, because I'm not sure I could survive all this right now without it." I took a few deep breaths before returning to my story.

"I still refused to live with my father. Even though the cops had hauled me there several times, I hadn't spoken a word to him since Mom's funeral. I went to stay with Kevin. I don't know why the hell he accepted me back into his life, but I'm thankful he did. He helped me stay clean, and made sure I took my Zoloft every day. If it wasn't for him, I probably would have gone right back to where I had been." I cried for a long time while Vittorio held me. I was surprised at how easy it was to tell him everything. Not once during my confession had a judging look crossed his face.

I choked on my sobs, knowing I had to come clean.

Vittorio pulled away slightly and studied my face. "What else is there, mio amore?"

CHAPTER TWENTY-SEVEN

I took a deep breath, trying to stop my tears. "I have to tell you something, and it's going to upset you. Please, if you can, let me finish before you say anything. And please believe that when I say I love you, I mean it more than anything."

"I do believe you. I feel the love, but I also feel your fear."

"I haven't been completely honest with you." I paused, scared to say the next part. "I didn't know you, had no idea who you were, no idea what a wonderful person you are, and never dreamed I'd fall so deeply in love with you. You're amazing, and I hate myself for what I've done. I want you to understand how much I hate it.

"I'm a private investigator. I went to The Chapel looking for my client's runaway daughter. It should have been a simple case, but then I met you."

"You told me you were in between jobs. Why did you lie?" His eyes narrowed, jaw clenched.

"I didn't want anyone to know I'm a P.I. If the girl didn't want her mother to find her, I figured her new friends would know that, and no one would talk to a P.I. Her mom is really worried about her, and I wanted to be as cautious as possible to avoid blowing a chance to find her. I had this strong feeling that there was more to the story than I or my client knew."

Vittorio sat up in bed, legs over the side facing away from me, shoulders tense.

I tentatively rested a hand on his shoulder, and he jerked away as if I shocked him. I recoiled, hurt by his reaction, even though I understood it.

"I wasn't supposed to fall in love with you. But I did, and everything was so good, and you're so perfect, I got caught up in it and didn't know how to stop it. I'm so sorry, Vittorio. I'm so sorry." I cried, and he said nothing. Finally, I moved. I knelt on the floor in front of him, lay my head on his knees clasping his hands and cried. "I'm so sorry. I know you must hate me now. I understand if you never want to see me again. But is there any way you can forgive me? I didn't know what I was getting into. I wasn't supposed to meet you, but then you found me, and I love you, and I can't stand the thought of losing you, but if you tell me to leave, I'll go. I'll never bother you again."

I dissolved into uncontrollable sobbing, and still, Vittorio said nothing. I held his hands tightly as if that would prevent him from leaving. I knew it wouldn't. Nothing would. I didn't deserve him.

After a while, he pulled his hands from mine, and I felt a tentative touch on my hair. I didn't move, didn't breathe for fear of scaring him away. Then Vittorio's arms were around me. "I'm so sorry. I love you. Please don't leave me," I cried. I clung to him, still unsure if he would leave or not.

Vittorio pulled me to my feet in front of him. "Mio amore, please calm down. I will not leave you."

"You won't?" I looked at him with wide eyes.

"No. I love you far too much, and feel how sorry you are. I am deeply hurt, though. It will be a while before I can fully trust you again."

"I know. I'll do whatever I can to regain your trust."

"I want you to tell me the full truth about yourself."

I sat back on the bed next to him, taking deep breaths. Through my sobs, I said, "Everything I told you was true. The only part I left out was my job. When I was arrested for the robbery, Jerry, the cop on the case, saw something in me and helped me. Kevin helped, too, but Jerry hooked me up with my psychiatrist. He convinced me to go to college. I got my associate degree in criminal justice. I didn't know what to do with my life. I was so

108

lost, so I just followed him. I was a cop for two years, but I hated it. Jerry and I had a falling out when I quit, and I haven't talked to him since."

"Tell me about this girl you're supposed to find."

"Her name is Courtney. She's nineteen, an art student at St. Louis Community College. She made friends with some Goths and her mom didn't like the way she changed. She mentioned a girl named Miriam, and someone named Elizabeth that her daughter seemed to idolize. I wonder if it's the Elizabeth we know."

Vittorio's eyes sparked. I wondered if he knew Courtney, but wasn't going to ask just then. Pushing him right now could make things worse.

I pulled my knees to my chest and began crying again. "I don't know if I'll ever be able to forgive myself."

"You must try. If you want me to forgive you, you must first forgive yourself."

CHAPTER TWENTY-EIGHT

Vittorio left me in bed to sleep. I didn't want him to leave me alone, but was scared to ask for more from him. I let him go, and must have fallen asleep almost as soon as he left. The day's training and emotional outpouring had exhausted me.

I didn't sleep well, and woke several times, always disappointed not to find Vittorio next to me. Finally, I could attempt sleep no more, weary though I was, so went to find Vittorio.

The door to his study was closed. I gave a soft knock, hoping both that he was and was not in there. I wanted to see him, but if I did, he would have the opportunity to change his mind and tell me to leave and never come back. To tell me he hated me. Or worse, that he'd been mistaken about loving me.

He called for me to come in so softly I might have imagined it.

I slowly opened the door, but didn't enter.

Vittorio sat at his desk, head in his hands. He did not look up.

I did not move.

After long moments of silence, I turned to go. "I shouldn't have bothered you."

As I began pulling the door shut behind me, Vittorio called out, "Wait."

I stopped, but did not turn around.

"Sit down."

I almost sat on the floor, right there in the doorway, but realized that would be silly. He must mean for me to sit in a chair. But had he told me to jump off a building, I would have if it meant he wouldn't leave me. My brain really wasn't working properly, my thoughts a mess of pain and regret.

"Clavius was right. I was blinded by my love for you."

"But I'm not trying to steal anyone's position. I only want your love."

"That may be, but you lied to me. How do I know if anything you told me was the truth? It's vital that we are careful about who we trust with knowledge of the coven. I have told everything to someone who was not honest with me."

"Can't you look into my heart? I've nothing else to hide." I clenched my hands in my lap, silently praying for him to believe me.

"I am frightened to." He finally looked up at my face, and I saw that his eyes were red.

I wanted to hang my head in shame, but feared not meeting his gaze would be a sign I had more to hide.

Vittorio looked away first. Only then did I bow my head and give in to silent tears.

"I know Courtney."

I jerked my head up to look at him. "You do?"

He nodded, face blank, but tightness around his lips and eyes showed it was a struggle for him to maintain that blankness. "Miriam has been a member of the coven for several years. She brought Courtney to us a few months ago. At first, Clavius told her to leave, but Miriam insisted she be allowed to hang around."

"And Clavius listened to a twenty year old?"

"Elizabeth is Miriam's aunt. She convinced Clavius, though it is a bit strange."

I drew in a sharp breath, eyes wide. "Does Courtney know about magic?"

"I do not believe so. It is the most important secret among us. Miriam is impulsive, but she idolizes her aunt, and would not risk Clavius' anger by telling Courtney. She does know of our beliefs, and wants to join the coven."

"Is Courtney okay?" Even amidst my own guilt, I feared

having to tell Ms. Carmen something bad had happened to her daughter.

"She is safe. She has been staying at Miriam's apartment."

"Will you introduce me to her?" Focusing on the case was easier than dealing with my emotions.

"I will. But you are right, it must seem natural. I do not talk to her much, but she has made her hatred of her mother clear. It will have to seem like a chance meeting at The Chapel."

"Thank you. I have to call her mother and let her know Courtney is alright." I almost darted out of the room, but stopped at the doorway. I turned and looked at Vittorio. His face was wistful. When I opened my mouth to ask why, the neutral expression returned. I left without another word, wanting to know what was on his mind, yet fearing it at the same time. He told me about Courtney; that must be a positive sign that he was going to give me another chance.

CHAPTER TWENTY-NINE

I spent most of the next day reading some books on witchcraft I found in Vittorio's study while he was at work. Ms. Carmen had been thankful to hear her daughter was safe, even at o'dark thirty. I never did bother to see what time it was after my late night conversation with Vittorio. I hoped I would get to meet Courtney soon, and set to work on convincing her to return home, or at least to call her mother.

"Get ready to go out. Courtney will be at The Chapel tonight."

I jumped, not having heard him arrive home, cringing at the command in his words. But what did I expect? A passionate greeting, all hurt from the night before forgotten? Setting the book aside, I left the study to get dressed, not looking at Vittorio, not wanting to see the pain that must be on his face.

Vittorio sat on the bed waiting for me when I got out of the shower. I felt more naked than I ever had and scrambled to find a robe. He had not changed from his work clothes, just removed the jacket and tie.

Once safely covered, I didn't know what to do, couldn't move, rooted just outside the bathroom door. What did he want from me?

Vittorio stood and came to me. He stood inches away, then wrapped his arms around me.

I froze. That was the last thing I had expected.

"Mio amore, relax."

He called me mio amore. That called forth a whole new wave of tears as I sank into his arms and clung to him as if he were the only thing keeping me alive.

He scooped me into his arms and carried me to the bed. "Mio amore, do not cry. I told you I will not leave you."

"I know, but I don't understand why not. I'd deserve it if you did. I keep expecting at any moment you're going to change your mind."

"I will be honest, I had thought about it, but I cannot stand the thought of living without you."

"I know, and I understand. I told you I'll do anything you ask."

"In that case, please stop crying. You are far more beautiful when you smile."

I couldn't help but smile at that.

"There, much better," he said, and kissed away my tears.

The feel of his lips on my face called to my power. I had let my guard down, and it rushed out of me toward Vittorio. This time, however, it hit a steel wall with such a force it physically jolted me. When I brought it back under control Vittorio explained.

"I suspected your emotions might cause you to lose control. Normally, my shield would not be so strong against you, but my pain and anger helped strengthen it."

"I'm sorry."

"You have apologized enough, Elena. It is time to start rebuilding what you destroyed." His words were harsh, but no harsher than my self-hatred. "Now, we really must get ready for tonight. Samuel confirmed that Courtney would be there."

"How does he know?"

"For some reason I do not understand, he has taken quite an interest in her."

"You mean, like, romantically?"

"I believe so."

"Does every man in the coven date younger girls?"

That earned me a grin. "No, mio amore, they do not. You are a rare creature. I honestly do not know what Samuel sees in Courtney, but she seems quite flattered by the attention of an older man.

"Now, get dressed." He kissed me. The intensity of his shields told me he hadn't completely forgiven me yet, but that was okay. He kissed me, and called me his love again.

CHAPTER THIRTY

Courtney sat next to Samuel on a love seat at The Chapel. Her mother was right; I barely recognized her from the picture she had given me. But I had a good idea what to look for in people, knew to look at the features and not the overall appearance. Her bottom lip was slightly fuller than the top, her button nose a little too short. She was a cute girl. Yes, cute was the word the came to mind. Next came "pretty," but I imagined her playing an adorable little mouse in a childhood play.

Her photograph revealed her to be the girl next door. Flesh and blood showed her as very cyber-Goth. A chain strung from her nostril to the cartilage at the top of her left ear. Three more silver hoops glinted in each of her ears, which were showcased by unruly bright pink pigtails. She wore a black corset that gave the illusion of more chest than she truly had and a black micro skirt that would give the world a show if she moved carelessly. Pink leg warmers that looked like a shaggy dog had been skinned to make them stretched from her ankles to just above her knees.

She threw her head back and laughed, loud and seductive, at something Samuel had said.

I rolled my eyes at Vittorio; she was trying way too hard.

Samuel lightly stroked her neck, and she shivered under the touch. The adoration in her eyes made it plain that she was in love with him - or thought she was. Beneath the sexuality of her outfit, I thought she might be a virgin, and despised Samuel for preying on her.

Courtney studied me and smiled. The smile reached her eyes,

and confidence radiated from her. I had expected her to be unsure of herself, lost, looking for meaning in her life as a runaway, but she knew exactly what she wanted and what she was doing. She wanted in the coven, and saw Samuel as her way in. The love was an act, so good an act that it had even fooled me.

Vittorio spoke first. "Courtney, I would like to introduce you to my love, Elena."

She shook my hand with a firm grip, impressing and shocking me even more. "Nice to meet you, Elena."

"I think we'll leave you ladies to talk for a while," Samuel said, standing to give me his seat, then walked to the other side of the balcony with Vittorio.

"How'd you snag Vittorio?" Courtney asked me. No beating around the bush for this girl.

"I honestly don't know." It was mostly truth. Had it not been for our power, I really wouldn't know.

"Is he going to bring you into the coven?"

"Maybe. I'm still learning about it, so I'm not even sure I want to join."

"Why wouldn't you want to be part of something like that?" She raised her eyebrows.

"Like what?" I asked.

"A family who accepts you no matter what?"

"I haven't been big on family in quite a while. Just more people to screw you over."

Seeming to sense she was on thin ice, she changed the subject. What had this girl been through to give her such a strong character at such a young age? "So what do you do?"

I decided to be honest with her. Courtney obviously wouldn't take bullshit from anyone, and I sensed that playing it straight with her would get me further than playing coy. "I'm a private investigator."

Her eyes widened and she took deep breaths to control whatever emotion that conjured in her.

"I'm going to be honest with you, Courtney. Your mother hired me to find you. She's worried sick about you."

"You can't make me go back home. I'm nineteen. That makes me legally an adult."

"I know, and I'm not going to make you. But you should at least call your mom and let her know you're okay."

"Why should I? I hate her, and she hates me."

I grabbed her arm without thinking. "You don't know how lucky you are to have a mother who loves you as much as she does. Don't you ever let me hear you say you hate her again."

"What the hell? Get your hands off me," Courtney snarled.

"I would give anything to have my mother alive. Anything. And here you are, mother alive and worried about you, acting like an ungrateful little snot." I let her go, and she just stared at me.

"I'm sorry," she whispered.

"Don't apologize to me. Apologize to your mother."

Courtney stood up, walked to Samuel and said something to him, then left. I hoped she was going outside to call her mom, and that I hadn't made a gigantic mess of things with her.

CHAPTER THIRTY-ONE

It had been several days since I had been home, so Vittorio took me there when we left The Chapel.

He walked me to the door, where we stood awkwardly for several moments. I felt like a teenager on her first date, wondering if she should kiss the boy, or wait for him to kiss her, or to run inside before anything could happen.

"I know my place isn't fancy, but, would you like to stay here tonight? I mean, you don't have to if you don't want to…" I trailed off.

He pulled me close to him. "Mio amore, it will take time for me to trust you completely again, and for the hurt to go away, but I still long to feel you close to me."

Once inside, I realized just how uncomfortable this must be for Vittorio. For one thing, he had nothing to change into, and while his outfit was stunning, I was willing to bet it wasn't the most comfortable thing to wear.

"I have some workout shorts that might fit you, if you want to try them, and a large t-shirt."

"Thank you," he said.

I searched through my dresser and found the shorts. "The bathroom's right around the corner."

He took the shorts without a word.

I changed into a red silk nightgown and lay in bed, waiting for Vittorio, tired, but too tense to think about sleep. I opened my eyes when I felt him in the doorway. My shorts barely fit him and looked as if they would tear at the seams. He knelt by the foot of the bed and laid a kiss on my ankle. My body tingled as he moved up my leg, gently planting kisses the entire way. He stopped at the hem of my nightgown and moved to my other leg, working his way up. Next, he kissed my fingertips, hand, and arm, ending at my neck, drawing a soft moan from me. Still, he continued, across my chest, always staying just at the line of my nightgown, teasing. My heart raced and my breath came fast. When he finally kissed my lips, I put my arms around him, pulling him to me. I wrapped my legs around his waist, using my eyes to wordlessly beg him for more. He stopped and gazed into my eyes. "What do you want?"

"You," I breathed and pulled him to me again. My hands explored the muscles of his back, dipped below the waistline of the shorts, then back up. My body ached for him. I gently let my power go to him and felt his answer.

We knelt on the bed; he pulled my nightgown over my head, and I pushed the shorts down. I cried out as he pressed against me.

When he entered me, it was unlike anything I had ever felt. Our powers truly became one, as did our bodies. I felt his emotions, the years of pain, the abandonment from his parents, his gratitude to Dr. Fondazione, his brotherly love for Samuel, the hurt my betrayal caused him, and on top of it all, the pureness of his love for me. Tears came to my eyes.

I felt his power tug at my soul, but it was not the tearing away he described. It was gentle, exploring, loving. I welcomed it in, invited it to find all it could about me. It hesitated, cautious about what it would find. There were no more lies, though, and my soul told the power as much, as it swept through me. I let it see my regret and sorrow, and love.

The misty green and amber of our power surrounded us, encasing us in protective, healing warmth.

When we finished, Vittorio collapsed on top of me. The weight of his body on mine was magnificent. I never wanted him to move. I held him, gently kissing his neck and shoulder because I loved the feel of his skin against my lips. Our powers lingered, swirling around us in an almost tangible mist until they faded.

"That was incredible," I whispered.

Vittorio propped himself on one elbow to look into my eyes. "Yes, mio amore, it was better than I ever could have dreamed." He rolled onto his back, and I lay my head on his chest, knowing the healing had begun.

"I'm going to make some coffee and see what I can scrounge up for breakfast. What do you like?" I asked when we woke the next morning.

"You," Vittorio said, kissing my back.

I sighed happily. "You've already had me."

"In that case, you decide."

Kevin walked in as I was frying bacon and scrambling eggs. I wasn't much of a cook, but breakfast I could handle. "Breakfast and your fancy robe. What's the special occasion? Have you finally decided you view me as more than a brother-type?"

"Keep dreaming. I'm a new woman, Kevin." We heard the shower turn on upstairs.

"Oh, I think I get it." He went to look out the front window to see Vittorio's car parked out front. "He's upstairs, huh?"

"Yep." I smiled.

"Okay, then, I'll be on my way. Wouldn't want to ruin your lovers' breakfast."

"You might have to rethink coming and going as you please. It might get a bit awkward."

"I always imagined my first threesome being with two girls, but maybe if you get me drunk enough…" He wiggled his eyebrows up and down.

"Go away, Kevin."

CHAPTER THIRTY-TWO

When we finished training for the day, Vittorio offered to make dinner. "I appreciate it, but I don't have much food in the house. I don't cook much, so frozen dinners are about the extent of what I have, aside from breakfast stuff. Feel free to scrounge in the fridge, but I doubt you'll find much of use in there."

"I could go to the grocery store." His eyes sparkled.

"Oh, right. I'm going to stay here, though. I want to fill Kevin in on what's going on with the coven. For one, he stopped by while you were in the shower this morning. And since he lives right next door, I think he deserves to know in case it gets ugly."

"Why don't you invite him over for dinner? I would like to get to know him better, and I think he was a little put off the last time we met," Vittorio said as he scanned my nearly-empty cabinets.

I wrapped my arms around him from behind. "Thank you, Vittorio."

"For what?"

"For including Kevin. For understanding how important he is to me. For last night. For loving me."

He turned to embrace me. "Mio amore, you do not have to thank me for those things. But if you do, I should thank you for last night, as well. I saw how strongly you regret what you did. Seeing that helped to begin healing the hurt."

After a few minutes, I forced myself to pull away. "Okay, well, I'll be here waiting for you. I love you."

When Vittorio left, I went to talk to Kevin. "Wanna come over for dinner?"

"Not if you're cooking," he said, eyes never leaving his favorite shoot 'em up video game on the TV.

"I'm not, so you'll be safe. Vittorio is going to cook." I went to the kitchen to get a beer for Kevin. Maybe it would convince him to say yes.

"What's he going to cook? All you have is frozen dinners."

"He's at the grocery store right now. And I didn't ask what he's making."

"As long as you two don't go all wonky on me again." He popped open the beer and took a long drink.

"We won't. I have much better control now."

"Sure you do. That's not how it sounded last night."

"You heard us?" I covered my face.

"The place is old; it doesn't have the thickest walls." He glanced at me briefly with a raised eyebrow.

"Oh, God," I said into my hands, still covering my face.

"Don't worry, I won't make fun of you. Much." He poked my side.

"Maybe you should have dinner by yourself tonight." I stood to leave.

"I already accepted, so you can't take it back now."

"Oh, fine. So listen, I need to talk to you."

"Not about last night, I hope." Kevin made a gagging noise.

"Of course not. You know I told you about kind of being the cause of that power struggle in the coven?"

He nodded, still playing his game.

I took the controller from his hands and paused it. "Well, it took a turn for the worse. They're trying to force Vittorio out. They probably want me far away, too." I told him about my battle with Elizabeth.

"Jesus, Elena, you have to get out of here. What's wrong with you, playing house, while your life is in danger?"

"Calm down, Kevin. I didn't say anything about my life being in danger. I'm perfectly safe for now, and Vittorio will protect me.

And Kevin, this has nothing to do with you. If things get ugly, I want you to stay out of it. I don't want you to get hurt because of me."

"Yeah, right, like I'm going to leave you alone to fight the bad guys." He reached for the controller, his signal this conversation was over.

I held it out of reach. "I can fight them more effectively than you can."

"So what? I'm not going to abandon you."

"It's safer that way."

"I don't care." I stared at Kevin for a minute before accepting he would not agree to stay out of this.

"Fine." I glared some more before completely giving up.

"Did you at least tell him the truth about yourself?"

"Yes." I tossed the controller on his couch before leaving. Hiding my fear behind anger was one of my better talents.

CHAPTER THIRTY-THREE

After meditating to calm my anger at Kevin's stubbornness, I decided to clean the kitchen. It wasn't dirty, but the thought of dinner with the two men in my life brought on a serious case of nerves. Kevin could be extremely antagonistic when he wanted to be, and I hoped he'd be on his best behavior.

The phone ringing startled me. It was Ms. Carmen.

"Elena, what did you say to my daughter?"

"Why? Is something wrong?" I worried Courtney had complained about me grabbing her arm and telling her off.

"No, she came home!" I heard the smile in her voice.

"That's wonderful news!"

"She said she'd stay if I stop yelling at her about her new look and friends."

I wanted to tell her she had nothing to worry about, but it would be a lie. I didn't know Miriam, but Elizabeth was trouble, and not a good role model for a young girl. "Ms. Carmen, I learned a little more about the coven Courtney mentioned, and I don't think it's anything for you to worry about. Your daughter isn't even involved with it." Technically, that was the truth; Clavius wouldn't let her in. Yet.

"Are you sure?"

"Pretty sure. She might just be going through a phase." That was as far as I was willing to stretch the truth in order to comfort Ms. Carmen. I'd done the job she hired me for. She wasn't paying me to play therapist.

"Well, if you say so. I'm just glad to have her home and know she's safe. Thank you so much."

"You're welcome. If I can ever be of assistance with anything else, you know my number."

Unease washed through my body as I hung up the phone. Courtney was stubborn. Why had she gone home so easily? My words may have caused her to rethink her hatred of her mother, but I doubted they would have caused such a sudden change and convince her to go back home. Something wasn't right.

"You are thinking too hard, mio amore," Vittorio said.

I dropped my cell phone.

"Did I startle you?" He set grocery bags on the counter.

"I didn't hear you come in."

"What has you so deep in thought?"

I told him of my conversation with Ms. Carmen while helping him unpack the groceries.

"It does seem odd, but try not to worry. You can be very persuasive when you want to be."

"Is that so?" I asked, and then kissed him.

"A late dinner, then?" Vittorio said, lips just above my neck, his breath sending shivers down my spine.

Vittorio made fabulous tortellini for dinner. To my surprise, Kevin accepted a glass of wine with dinner and said he liked it. "I've usually only had cheap stuff from a box at parties. Guess I've never had good wine before," he explained.

"I am pleased you like it," Vittorio said. "Elena made sure I picked up some beer for you as well."

"Thanks, I appreciate that." Kevin finished the glass and poured some more for all of us. "So Elena said you graduated college when you were twenty. That's pretty quick."

"Yes. Once I was released from the hospital, I was determined not to lose any more time. I studied almost constantly and took a heavy course load."

"I'm impressed man. I hated school."

"It is not for everyone. But I wanted to prove to myself that I could do something worthwhile. My parents, then my doctors, had made me feel so worthless, and even at that young age I realized how short life is. Maybe it was because of what I'd been through that brought me to that realization. I didn't really know how to do that, so I just studied as hard as I could. My parents wouldn't answer my calls or letters to see that I was truly better, but at least I proved it to myself."

"Why business?"

"As much as I admired Julian for what he did and how he'd helped me, medicine didn't interest me. As I said, I didn't really know what I wanted to do specifically, and business seemed to be the most versatile course of study. Between that and Julian teaching me how to control my power, how to be a good man, I think I've done well. I hope I have, at least."

"Well, seeing how well you treat Elena, and how well you've done in your job, I'd have to agree with you," Kevin said, taking another bite of tortellini.

"How did you get into working on cars?"

"My dad is a mechanic. I spent as much time as my mom would let me at his shop, watching and helping when he'd let me. She hated it - both of us coming home to dinner covered in grease. Every weekend he'd take me to little local car shows, or we'd be working on his old '57 Chevy. Mom always tried to get me to read more, encouraged me to find something else to do with my life, but I was good with cars. I loved it. I never wanted to do anything else."

"That is great that you found your passion at such a young age."

"I'd like to open my own shop someday. I don't want to work for someone else my whole life. That's why I live in this dump. I could afford a nicer place, but who cares? I'd rather save my money. Plus I can keep an eye on Elena here."

"You never told me you wanted your own shop!" I said.

"Yeah, well, I thought you'd laugh at me," Kevin said, looking down at the table.

"Why on earth would I do that?"

"I don't know, so many small businesses fail."

"I know a thing or two about business," Vittorio said. "I would be happy to help you if you want."

"That would be great man, thanks!"

When we finished the rest of the wine, Kevin helped me clear the dishes. "I may not understand this power stuff, but Vittorio's okay. He has my seal of approval."

"Thanks Kevin," I said, and then we returned to the living room.

"I'm going to head home, have to be up early for work tomorrow," Kevin said. "Thanks again for offering to help, Vittorio."

"Anything for a friend of Elena's."

Vittorio reached out to shake Kevin's hand, and then Kevin pulled him into a one-armed man hug. I tried to suppress a laugh at Vittorio's awkwardness.

"Kevin is a good man. I am glad you have had him to take care of you," Vittorio said as we went up to the bedroom.

"Me too," I said, falling into bed. It was early, but the night had been my equivalent of bringing the boyfriend home to meet the parents. I fell asleep almost as soon as I was in bed.

CHAPTER THIRTY-FOUR

The next day, we went back to Vittorio's for more training. His study looked like something straight out of an exclusive 19th century men's club in a movie. The walls were lined with floor to ceiling bookshelves, all filled with books; most of the books looked old. A large mahogany desk sat toward the back of the room and was covered with books and papers.

"I hold the position of the La Guardia, the Guardian in my coven, which is the second highest ranking. Traditionally, La Guardia was also responsible for the safety of the Sacerdotessa, though that is mainly a ceremonial role now. We are led by the Sacerdotessa, and Sacerdote, who represent the Goddess and God in rituals."

"Why all the Italian words?"

"My coven was started by Italian immigrants here in Boston in what is now Little Italy. They kept many of the Old Ways when they moved to this country."

"Is there a female second in command?" I asked, trying hard to commit all this to memory.

"It is not second in command, exactly, but yes. Dama D'onore, The Maiden assists the Sacerdotessa during rituals and maintains the altar. Elizabeth holds that position, and she is now afraid of losing it to you. She was the woman in the group the other night."

Now I understood why she hated me so much. "Why did Clavius make you the La Guardia? Isn't Samuel's power strong, too?"

"Yes, but our powers are different. Clavius believed mine to be more suitable for the position of the La Guardia. Recently, however, Clavius has become very close with Samuel. They claim it is simply because they have both suffered the loss of a loved one, but I wonder if there is something more to it, if Clavius now wishes he had made Samuel La Guardia." Vittorio looked distant, as if trying to figure out some mystery.

"His mother," I said, remembering the shrine I'd stumbled upon in his house.

Vittorio nodded.

Wanting to get back to training, I asked, "What do you really do? Is it like in the movies where you all stand around chanting and burning candles and all that stuff?"

"Yes and no. Hollywood tends to glamorize a lot of things. I suppose some would see witchcraft as glamorous, simply because it is so different from what most are used to. It is simply a religion, though, according to many who practice; there are rites, rituals and holidays. When you really look at the practices of the coven, many of the basic beliefs are similar to those of mainstream Christianity. Treat others as you want to be treated, respect for the Divine. It is true that we worship multiple gods. The point is, we are peaceful. What you see in movies often paints witches in a very bad light, which is a pity, because most people do not understand what we truly believe. Yes, we perform rituals, sometimes elaborate ones with many items required. They are similar to Christian prayer, though. We ask for goddess' or god's blessing; we thank them when good things happen. We simply base our beliefs on the more tangible aspects of the earth spirits rather than an image of some bearded man sitting on a throne in the clouds." Vittorio walked to a bookshelf and pulled down two books; one large and old, the other smaller and newer looking.

I laughed at that comparison. "I like the idea of worshipping the earth. I've never been keen on the big guy in the sky smiting us when we screw up and all the petty rules supposedly laid out in the Bible."

"There are rules in witchcraft, but they might be described more accurately as guidelines for living, and they should be common sense. Like I said, treat others as you want to be treated, respect mother earth; these are things any decent person should do on their own anyway." He handed me the books, then sat again. "You can read these. They should help you understand more and be a good reference. I do not expect you to remember everything all at once."

"If there is a power struggle in your coven, where would I fit in?"

"I hate to use the terms win or lose, but that is the simplest way to explain it. If I win, there is a chance I will be able to take position of Sacerdote. You would then be in place for Sacerdotessa." Vittorio reached out to hold my hands.

"Wow." That was way more responsibility than I wanted. I fought to maintain my cool, shoving panic down before it overwhelmed me.

"The other possibility is that I will remain the La Guardia, but you will have the opportunity to replace Elizabeth as Dama D'onore. You do not have to accept, of course."

"But?" What more could there be than the possibility of the highest position in the coven?

"If you do not, you will be viewed as weak, which will put you in danger from our enemies. I am truly sorry, mio amore. I wish I did not have to put you in this position."

I didn't tell him I agreed. He probably knew already.

CHAPTER THIRTY-FIVE

Vittorio left the study briefly after receiving a phone call from Samuel. I used the time to ponder what he told me. Aspects of witchcraft appealed to me, something to replace the feelings of loss and abandonment from my childhood. My Catholic upbringing seemed so cold to me, and when I tried going back to church after cleaning up, the congregation greeted me with judgment and scorn rather than the acceptance and forgiveness they preach. Religion lost its appeal, but I now wondered if perhaps this could be the path for me. The position of Sacerdotessa seemed daunting, though; it could be more responsibility than I was ready for.

Vittorio returned, brow furrowed. "It seems as if we were correct; those who would stand against me are already organizing an effort to force me out of the coven. Your display the other night frightened them even more than I suspected. I wanted to spend more time this evening working with you to control your power, but need to go to The Chapel now. I must maintain a strong presence."

"Why do you have to go? What's going to happen?" I stood and went to him.

"Most likely, nothing. It will be a night like any other, with drinking and socializing. But if I am absent, it will be viewed as a sign of weakness or fear by some. It is all mind games. I find it quite silly, but unfortunately, must play along."

"What about me?" I didn't want to be left behind.

"That is your decision, mio amore. I will not ask you to decide on what we talked about, but I do need to know if you will stand by my side through this. I wish I could change what is about to happen. Unfortunately, I cannot."

"I told you I would stick with you." Why were men so dense sometimes?

"Yes, but I do not want to assume you agree to be part of this fight."

I stood to face him, as much as I could, being so much shorter. "Vittorio, I love you. Whatever you need, if I can do it, I will. If that is standing by your side through this, that's what I'll do."

He embraced me. "You cannot possibly understand what that means to me, mio amore."

"Isn't that what people do when they love each other?"

"Yes, but I have not had much support in my life such as you say you will give me. It makes it all the more precious, especially coming from you."

I understood what he meant. It was like how much I appreciated Kevin never writing me off. The gratitude and love in Vittorio's eyes made me want to fly to the moon and back if that's what he needed. My heart raced with love for him. He trusted me to stand by him and help him in this fight. Me, who he had only just learned had deceived him. I would die before letting him down.

In keeping with Vittorio's desire to show a unity of our power, I wore the purple gown he bought me, and he again wore the fantastic tux. I had discovered the last time it had a satin feel to it. It was so soft I had a hard time keeping myself from stroking his arm or back to feel the fabric. Okay, so maybe that wasn't the only reason I had a hard time keeping my hands off him. I tried to behave, though, because I knew I would need every ounce of control I had, and still wasn't sure it would be enough.

As we ascended the stairs to the balcony, I felt his power gently reach out from his body. "What are you doing?" I whispered.

"Simply a show of strength."

"Can I help?"

"Not tonight. You need more training, and I want you to conserve your strength."

"Won't that make us look weak?"

"Perhaps, but it is a risk I am willing to take. If things get out of control later, and you have depleted your energy on a display such as this, it will make us look even weaker. If anyone comments on it, tell them they are not worth it for you to expend any energy on."

"Well, that's the truth. From the little you've told me, I wouldn't give these people the time of day if I had any choice in the matter." I shook my head.

"I agree, but unfortunately, we do not have a choice."

When we reached the top of the stairs, we found Samuel sitting in an armchair facing an empty love seat he had saved for us. Everyone turned to stare at us, but Vittorio kept walking as if we three were the only people in the room.

I tried to follow suit, but couldn't resist surveying the occupants from the corner of my eye. I was uncomfortable, unused to situations where tension so completely saturated the air.

The three from the other night sat at the opposite side of the balcony from us. When we sat down, I asked Vittorio their names, even though I already knew Elizabeth's. She had been with Samuel six months ago. It did not seem as if they were still together, but that fact made me even more suspicious of him. Or perhaps that is what had driven them apart. Or maybe her accompaniment to the art museum had been a friendly gesture. I would have to find out what their relationship was.

"Jonah, Neal, and Elizabeth. Elizabeth will have even more animosity for you, as she has been trying to win my affections for years, and I talk to her as little as possible."

"Great," I muttered. "And she thinks I'm trying to steal her position."

"This will not be easy, Elena," Samuel said. It seemed as if Vittorio had filled him in on some of our discussion while I was getting ready, but found I did not mind. All I cared about at that point was making it through the night without losing control of my power.

CHAPTER THIRTY-SIX

It was getting late; I was tired and hoped we could leave soon. So far, the night had been uneventful, and would even have been enjoyable were it not for the thickness of the atmosphere and little displays of power here and there. Elizabeth would throw a small spark of electricity at me, forcing me to fortify my shields to block it. My hopes crashed when I returned from the bathroom to find Vittorio and Samuel in a heated discussion with Jonah, Neal, and Elizabeth. An image in my head showed me standing next to Vittorio, my arm through his. It stopped me in my tracks when I realized that was what he wanted me to do. That was going to take some getting used to. More thoughts and images that weren't mine filled my head. Somehow, I knew they were Vittorio's, and I knew it was a warning that things might get ugly. My breath came fast and shallow as fear took hold of me; fear of an impending fight, and fear at Vittorio being able to invade my thoughts. Even though I knew he meant no harm by it, was trying to help even, I wasn't sure I liked it.

"Jonah, I have no intention of trying to take control of the coven. I do not want that responsibility," Vittorio said.

"I don't believe you. Why would you have introduced her into all this otherwise?" Jonah said.

"A man can want a woman for the pure reason of love alone, Jonah. I know that is a foreign concept to you, but please, try to understand it. I love Elena. Simple as that. There is no hidden purpose behind our relationship."

"How is it that you have so easily fallen in love with a woman you barely know?" Elizabeth asked.

Her power searched for me, and it stung my body. I resisted crying out in pain, and gently pushed back with my own power. The desire to slam it into her full force was strong, but I remembered what Vittorio said about rarely needing to use the full strength. Need and want were two different things, so I held back, but did put enough energy into it to hurt her.

"You little bitch," she said, and renewed her push against me, stronger this time. I sensed I was stronger than her, but did not have as much control. This could get ugly.

I half expected Vittorio to come to my rescue, but he didn't. *If you need me, I will be here, but you must try to do this on your own, mio amore. You must show Elizabeth your strength.* How the hell did I hear him so clearly in my head?

I don't understand this, and it makes it hard to concentrate, so please be quiet. I hoped he got my message, but didn't have time to worry about it as a million needles poked all over my body. Soon, I grew tired of the back and forth with Elizabeth. Trying to figure out what else I could do with my power to make her surrender, I remembered Vittorio telling me he threw a nurse across the room. I pushed back at her with electricity to give me a moment to concentrate, then pulled my power completely back. Focusing only on Elizabeth, I sent my power to her. She stumbled backwards. Her needles turned into knives in my body. I feared if I looked down I would be bleeding.

I closed my eyes and pictured her in the chair across the balcony, unable to move, and let my power go. When I opened my eyes, I saw what I hoped for. She was in the chair, struggling to stand. I threw the electric power at her for good measure, and she cried out in pain. This time, I did not stop. I knew it would not permanently injure her, but it must have hurt like hell.

Vittorio's arm on my shoulder brought me back to reality. "That is enough, Elena."

Elizabeth's face contorted in ugly pain. Had I done that? I

called my power back, frightened. What else could I do? What other horrible pain could I inflict? Success had clouded my mind, causing me to hurt Elizabeth more than was necessary. Would that happen every time?

From the looks on everyone's faces, including Vittorio's and Samuel's, I knew we had won this round. But at what price?

CHAPTER THIRTY-SEVEN

Vittorio scheduled dinner with Clavius the following evening. "I have told him about you during our training sessions, and he will know about last night. It is long past time that I introduce you to him. He can be quite intimidating, but do not let him make you feel small."

"I don't go well for intimidation. In case you forgot, Bryn warned me about you, and look where that got us."

"I hope you do not have the same reaction to Clavius," he said grinning.

"Clavius who?" I said, kissing Vittorio. "What do I wear to a meeting like this?"

"You should look stunning, yet unassuming, considering some of the members' fears. I believe the corset you wore the night we met will be perfect."

"And how do I act around this guy?" My stomach flip-flopped.

"Treat him as you would any other authority figure, with respect and deference, but there is no special protocol for this situation."

"Why haven't you introduced me sooner?"

"We have been busy with your training, and Clavius has not been as on top of matters as he once was. Not since Aerin died. But things are getting out of control. He must step up and control his coven."

A leader who no longer cared…that was a scary thought.

Dinner was at an expensive fondue restaurant on Delmar, a trendy area of town with the street lined with boutique shops, restaurants and bars for several blocks. When we arrived at the restaurant, Clavius was waiting for us. With light red hair and clear, pale skin, he looked no older than twenty-five, though if he was older than Vittorio, he must have been closer to forty-five.

He looked me up and down with piercing ice-blue eyes.

I slammed my shields into place, blocking his power from probing me, and instantly felt safer.

"So it is true. You are very powerful," Clavius said.

"How can you tell so soon?" I asked

"You have much to learn." He studied me, and I froze.

Vittorio came to my rescue. "Clavius, I would like to introduce you to my love, Elena."

Clavius took my hand from Vittorio and chastely kissed the back of it. "A pleasure to finally meet the woman who has stolen my Guardia's heart. I did not think it was possible."

"And I am pleased to meet the man who has taught my love all he knows," I said.

Clavius chuckled. "I cannot claim to have taught him everything he knows. He learned much before he came to me."

I did not expect Clavius to be humble, and assumed it was an act. "I'm sorry to hear about Aerin," I said. "I understand how it feels to lose someone you love." I didn't plan to tell Clavius my whole story, but I felt a sort of bond with people who lost someone close to them because of violence. It's nice to meet someone who understands what one has gone through.

"Thank you for your sympathies," he said, and I sensed it was sincere.

I nodded, and then waited out an awkward silence. Under Clavius' scrutiny, those moments seemed endless, and felt like a test of some sort.

"Shall we sit?" Clavius finally asked, looking pleased.

The hostess immediately brought us to a corner booth toward the back of the restaurant. It provided privacy, and I suspected it had been planned.

Clavius ordered a bottle of wine for us, and then we reviewed the menu in silence. I had never been able to afford to eat at the restaurant, but had heard about it. Meals consisted of salad, cheese fondue, meat fondue, and chocolate fondue for dessert. I let Vittorio order a meal for the two of us, and iced tea for me.

"Tell me, Elena, how did you manage to steal Vittorio's heart? Many women have tried over the years, but no one has succeeded," Clavius asked after we ordered and the waitress took our menus.

"I honestly don't know, but he has stolen mine as completely, which is just as strange. I'm not the type of girl to be swept off her feet by a pretty face."

"Vittorio tells me he suspects your power has something to do with it."

"Maybe," I said, unwilling to commit to the answer.

Clavius remained silent and raised an eyebrow at me.

"I don't understand it enough to know." That was true, and I didn't want to say too much. Clavius made me uncomfortable for a reason I couldn't quite pin down. I wanted to squirm in my seat like a schoolgirl being reprimanded by the principal, but forced myself to remain still.

"Interesting."

I reached for Vittorio's hand under the table, desperate for any encouragement I could get. He squeezed it, and whispered in my mind, *You are doing well, mio amore. Relax.*

I tried. Over the salad and cheese course, Clavius made small talk. I was beginning to relax just a little, but felt no more comfortable.

When the meat course came out - they brought pots of boiling broth and bite sized pieces of meat you were to cook in the pots yourself - Clavius got down to business. "So, Elena, Elizabeth tells me she fears you will try to usurp her position in the coven."

"She's wrong. I don't want anyone's position. I don't even know the ways of your religion." I was offended that so many people thought I was so power hungry. Why couldn't they understand I just wanted to be left alone?

"Yet you have power, and Vittorio has offered to teach you our ways." He speared a piece of meat and set the long fork carefully in the pot of broth.

"Yes, but I don't know if I will even want to join the coven."

"But you are very powerful," he insisted.

"If I could give up my power, I would."

Clavius' eyebrows raised and his eyes widened. "Really?"

"Yes. I've always believed in the possibility of magic, and sometimes wished to experience it myself, but now that I have, I would take that wish back. This is all a bit overwhelming. I'd rather keep to myself than have all this going on." I poked at a piece of meat, but had little appetite left.

"Yet Elizabeth fears you." His eyes never left mine.

"I can't help it if she's insecure. I tried to tell her I don't want her position, but she wouldn't listen to me."

"And your display of power against her made her even more fearful of you." Clavius pulled his fork from the pot and dipped his now cooked piece of meat into some sort of sauce.

"That was not my intention. I was only trying to protect myself." I took a sip of tea, my throat suddenly dry.

"And look how it backfired," Clavius said, spearing another piece of meat with his fork.

Vittorio was silent through this exchange, slowly eating while watching us. He squeezed my leg in reassurance.

"Are you saying you don't believe me?" I asked Clavius.

"I don't know what I believe. I do not know you well enough to make a decision on my beliefs about this."

"Clavius, you can believe Elena. I did not choose to love her so that I could bring her into the coven to take anyone's position. I did not choose to love her at all. My heart left me no choice in the matter. I love her for who she is, not because of her power," he said, putting his arm around my shoulders and kissing me on the cheek.

"But you said you thought her power had something to do with your love," Clavius said. It was not a question.

"Yes, I believe it is why I was initially drawn to her so strongly, but even if she had no power, I would still love her. She is a beautiful woman in every way and has no ill intent toward anyone. You can trust her, as I trust her."

Clavius studied Vittorio. "I can see you believe what you say. But that does not mean Elena has not fooled you of her intentions. Men are often deceived by beautiful women, besotted by their looks."

"I do not believe that I am, Clavius."

"Hmm." Clavius chewed his food thoughtfully for several minutes. "Very well. I will tell Elizabeth she has nothing to worry about. Do not prove me wrong." Clavius looked at me as he said the last part.

"I won't. I promise, I want nothing more than Vittorio's love." Relief that he finally believed me allowed me to relax just a little.

Clavius made more small talk over dessert, and I hoped I responded in the appropriate manner to his questions.

I took a deep breath of clean night air when we left the restaurant. A weight lifted from my shoulders now that Clavius was gone.

I sighed, sinking into the soft, comforting leather of Vittorio's Ferrari.

CHAPTER THIRTY-EIGHT

I saw Courtney at The Chapel more often over the next week, always with Samuel. Sometimes she seemed so young, so naive, but then I caught a glimpse of ruthlessness in her face, and knew she would stop at nothing to be brought into the coven.

"How are things with you and your mom?" I asked her one night while Vittorio and Samuel talked business.

"Alright, I guess. She doesn't nag me anymore, at least."

"She really does love you."

"I guess." She watched Samuel.

I realized the look in her eye was not love. It was closer to possessiveness.

"What?" she asked.

"You don't love him, do you?"

"Why do you care?" She crossed her arms over her chest.

"He's a friend, of sorts." I shrugged, still unsure how to classify Samuel. My power still did not trust him.

"That's high praises," she snorted.

"He is Vittorio's best friend."

"That still doesn't explain why you care whether I love him or not." She reached toward her ear as if to fidget with a metal addition, then stopped herself midway.

"I'm just trying to figure you out," I said.

"Why?"

"Curiosity. Maybe I like you." In reality, I hoped to figure out why she had gone home so easily. Her sudden change still didn't sit well with me.

"I don't see that it's any of your business," she said, then stood and walked to Samuel, interrupting his conversation with Vittorio with a very sensual kiss.

Vittorio left them to their kiss and sat next to me. "She leaves your conversations often. I am not sure she likes you, mio amore," Vittorio said.

"I can't figure her out. Why did she go home so easily?"

"Are you still worried about that? Do not let it bother you. We have bigger problems." He flicked his eyes toward Elizabeth. "She is planning something, but I do not know what."

"How do you know?" I played my hand along the back of his, never quite able to stop touching him when we were close.

"She seems to have given up on you, but I know her better than that. I have seen her like this once before."

"What do you mean?"

"Before she was Dama D'Onore, she worked hard to gain Aerin's affection. Aerin would not replace the woman who held the position at the time, and it seemed as if Elizabeth had given up on it. Then one day, the woman was found dead in her home, an apparent suicide. Elizabeth had a bullet proof alibi, but when Aerin appointed her as the Maiden, it seemed all too convenient, as it is too convenient for Elizabeth to simply ignore you now."

Icy fingers clutched my gut. "You think she's going to try to kill me?"

"I do not know, mio amore, but we must be careful of her and her trusted circle."

"You mean Neal and Jonah?"

"Yes."

I huddled close to Vittorio, and he held me tight. My job as a P.I. wasn't always safe, but I had never felt truly in fear of my life before.

Ms. Carmen was frantic when she burst into my office the next day. "Elena, someone has stolen my map!"

"I'm sorry, what happened?"

"Remember the map I told you about, the one that Samuel Porter wanted to buy?" She paced in front of my desk.

"Yes. Please, won't you sit down?" Her pacing fed into my already frayed nerves.

"It's gone! And Courtney hasn't been home in two days." She just about collapsed into an empty chair.

"Do you think she took it?" I slowly sipped my coffee, hoping if I remained calm she would follow suit.

"I don't know, but there was no break-in. I don't want to think that of my daughter, but it's the only thing I can think of. I have a security system on the house, and another in the room where I keep my artifacts. Can you find it, and her, for me?"

"Which is more important?" I sensed it was the map.

"My daughter, of course." She tried to feign offense, but I knew it was false.

"Why is this map so important?" I reached for a pen and notepad.

"Ponce de Leon drew it himself, which is why it is so sought after. Most people believe the Fountain of Youth to be located somewhere in the Caribbean. This map shows it to be on an island in the Gulf of Honduras, but the island doesn't seem to exist."

"Do you have the map insured?" I asked after making a note about the map.

"Of course I do, but why does that matter?"

"Just trying to gather all the facts, Ms. Carmen. Have you reported this to the police?"

"No. With the map and my daughter disappearing at the same time, I suspect she took it, and I don't want to involve the police. I don't want something like that to go on her record. You did such a good job of finding her the first time, I thought you could find her again."

I had some very solid ideas of where the map was, but didn't want to tell her anything until I was sure. "I'll find your daughter and ask her if she knows anything about it. You already know my rate. I'll be in touch." I stood and led her to the door, not in the mood for niceties. Her tone made it plain she was more worried about the map than her daughter this time.

CHAPTER THIRTY-NINE

When I left my office for the day, I took Ms. Carmen's file, which contained copies of the articles about the premiere. They would be proof to back up my suspicion that Samuel was somehow behind the theft. I knew Vittorio would not easily believe such a thing of his best friend.

While I walked back to my car, my power suddenly flared up. I stopped dead in my tracks, and had enough time to think 'something's wrong' before someone grabbed me from behind and covered my mouth. The person shoved me into the backseat of a car, causing me to hit my head on the window, and then tore out of the parking lot.

When I shook off the pain, I realized someone was in the backseat with me. It was Samuel. "What the hell?"

I tried to get away, but the rear door seemed to have childproof locks, and he tied my hands behind my back and draped some kind of amulet around my neck. "Now you won't be able to call to your precious Vittorio for help. That amulet will block you from using any of your powers."

I tried, but couldn't feel my connection to Vittorio. Shit. My Smith and Wesson Model 10 was in the holster at the small of my back. Before I could even think about trying to aim it with my hands tied, Samuel took it from me. I wondered how he had known about it, or if he was just being extra cautious.

Neal drove and Elizabeth sat in the front seat glaring at me. "Sounds like you've been having a lot of fun with Vittorio. He was supposed to be mine, you little bitch."

"Excuse me?" How the hell did she know about that? Had Vittorio told Samuel? He didn't strike me as the kiss and tell type.

"Your weak little friend told us."

Kevin! "What did you do to him?"

"He's alive; don't worry. Neal saw him go into your house and decided he might be useful."

They had been stalking me? "He wouldn't have told you anything on his own. What did you do to him?"

"Nothing that won't heal. A little torture is good for a person's character."

I was going to be sick.

My cell phone rang, and Samuel got it out of my purse. "Here's your little lovebird calling now. Why don't you talk to him?" Samuel flipped open the phone and held it to my ear.

"Elena, what is wrong? I cannot reach you with my thoughts."

"Get away from here. Leave town. Now. Just go. Don't worry about me."

Samuel backhanded me across the face.

"Please, just go," I sobbed.

"Elena, where are you?"

Samuel took the phone from my ear. "She's perfectly safe here with me, Vittorio. If you do as I say, that is. If you don't, we'll see if she holds up as well as her friend Kevin did."

A string of curses resonated from the phone. I never would have imagined my proper Vittorio capable of such language.

"You might want to calm down, friend. You don't know what will anger me. Now, here's what I want you to do. Meet me at The Chapel in an hour. I'll take you to Elena from there. And you better come alone."

"Don't do it, Vittorio!" I shouted, knowing it was hopeless.

Samuel backhanded me again; this time I tasted blood.

"You know I can control my power now. Stay away from them!" I yelled to Vittorio. Never mind the fact that the amulet somehow blocked my power. Vittorio didn't need to know that. I didn't care what happened to me. I just wanted to keep him safe.

"Your little pet is a brave one, my friend. What she isn't telling you is we've placed a power-blocking amulet on her. She's completely helpless. The Chapel. One hour." Samuel ended the call.

"You bastard. You backstabbing asshole. Vittorio trusted you." I spat in his face.

"All the worse for him. And you, it seems," he said, wiping the spit away with a handkerchief.

"I knew you were up to something, but Vittorio assured me I could trust you."

"Loyalty has always been his downfall. And now you're going to pay for his loyalty."

"And you're going to pay for stealing my man," Elizabeth said.

"He was never your man. You never had a chance in hell with him."

"Watch your mouth, slut," she said as she twirled a knife in her hands. "You wouldn't want to lose anything important, now, would you? What would your dear Vittorio think of you then?"

A woman scorned, men battling for power, and me in the middle of it all, defenseless. There was no way Samuel would let Vittorio waltz in and rescue me, so I was going to have to figure this one out on my own.

CHAPTER FORTY

Neal dropped Samuel off at The Chapel, and then drove through some winding country roads, leaving me completely lost. We ended up at a huge house in the middle of nowhere. I would have bet this was where they held the rituals. They dragged me into the basement. I expected to see some dungeon-like room with a concrete floor and drain in the middle, like in bad horror movies, and was surprised to find a nicely furnished basement instead. They took me into a large utility room, and I saw Kevin. "Oh my God, Kevin, are you okay?" That was a stupid question. Obviously, he wasn't. His face was badly beaten, and his right arm hung to his side at a grotesque angle.

"Elena?" His eyes were swollen nearly shut. Elizabeth was standing behind me, pushing me into the room. I snapped my head back as hard as I could to hit hers. She cried out and momentarily loosened her grip. It was enough for me to get away from her and run to Kevin. I hugged him as best I could with my arms tied behind my back and began crying.

"I'm so sorry, Kevin. This is all my fault."

Elizabeth caught up to me and backhanded me across the mouth, splitting my lip. I looked at her and saw her nose bleeding. Point for me, I thought, swallowing my own blood.

"You'll pay for this, bitch." She pulled me roughly to my feet then shoved me into a chair across the room from Kevin and tied me to it. She took out her knife and waved it in front of my face. "You're lucky Samuel said he wants you mostly unharmed for now. Otherwise, I'd cut up your pretty face."

I spat at her, which wasn't the brightest thing I'd ever done.

"Did you miss the part where I said 'mostly?' " She pressed the knife to my neck. That wouldn't be 'mostly,' so I tried to remain calm. That would kill me. I prayed she was more scared of Samuel than angry at me. Turned out she was. Mostly. She dragged the knife across my forearm, and then walked out of the room, my dripping blood a temporary goodbye gift.

"Kevin, I'm so sorry. I should have trusted my instinct about Samuel."

"Can't you use your power to get us out of here?"

"No. They put this amulet on me and it blocks everything." Burning pain shot through my arm. "I can't even communicate with Vittorio."

"So, we're just stuck here?"

"No, he's coming. He called after they grabbed me, and Samuel told him to meet him at The Chapel. I'm sure he'll bring him here. I just hope he can get us out of this without getting himself killed."

Footsteps came from the stairs. I prayed it was Vittorio, and then prayed it wasn't. Samuel entered the room first, followed by Vittorio. Neal had a strong grip on him, preventing him from coming to me. I guessed they didn't want to risk him taking the amulet off me.

"Elena, are you alright?"

"Yeah." I felt that my lip had swollen, and guessed my face was bruising from where Samuel slapped me. The bleeding seemed to have stopped on my arm, but when I looked down at it I saw it was covered in blood. "Mostly, anyway."

"Let her go. You have me now. You don't need her."

"Oh, but there you are wrong. We need her more than you. We only brought you here as a bit of extra incentive in case her darling Kevin wasn't enough."

"You have me, just let Kevin go!" I pleaded.

Elizabeth backhanded me. "No one is talking to you, tramp, so shut up."

Vittorio fought Samuel's grip, but couldn't break free. I was shocked. Vittorio was much larger than Samuel, and I knew how strong he was. Why couldn't he overpower him?

"I've given him a low dose of sedative so he can't fight me," Samuel said, as if reading my mind.

Elizabeth twirled her knife again. "Will you work with us?" Samuel asked.

"I don't even know what you want," I shouted. "Please, Vittorio, don't worry about me. Just get yourself out of here."

"Do you really think I would abandon you with these lunatics?" He continued struggling weakly against Samuel's grip.

I shrugged. "Not really. But I don't want you to get hurt."

"I'm getting impatient," Samuel said.

"Let her go," Vittorio said.

"I already told you. No. Asking again will only make me angrier," Samuel said. He threw Vittorio against the wall, his head making a sickening crack.

"I will not help you."

"Oh, really?" Samuel grinned maniacally. "Elizabeth." He nodded toward her.

She drew the knife across my other arm as Vittorio shouted wordlessly. I resisted crying out for his sake.

Samuel and Neal dragged him away, leaving Kevin and me alone with Elizabeth and her knife.

CHAPTER FORTY-ONE

"How about you help us?" Elizabeth lightly traced her knife down my arm. It scratched my skin, but did not draw blood.

"What do you want from me?" I tried to keep my voice steady.

"Samuel thinks you can translate a very old text he recently acquired."

I couldn't help but laugh at that. "He needs to do his research better. I don't speak any languages other than English." Maybe if I kept her talking, she'd forget about the knife she held. Yeah, and I was Mother Theresa.

"That you're aware of."

"Maybe if you'd quit being so damned cryptic, I could give you a proper answer." The pressure from the knife grew, drawing a thin line of blood.

"There's an ancient language that only one strega each century is able to read. Because of the strength of your power, Samuel thinks you may be that strega."

"And what am I supposed to translate?"

"A spell. Nothing more."

I had the feeling it was more than just a simple spell. Otherwise, why would they have had to kidnap and torture us? "If that's all it is, why do you need Vittorio?"

"You will need someone to guide you through the translation. Clavius has taught him about this language, though neither are able to read it. It will be easiest for him to guide you since you trust him."

"But why not just ask us? Why all this?"

"Maybe it's just more fun this way." She cut deep into my arm. Again, I managed to not cry out in pain.

"What's your answer?"

If the spell was as benign as she said it was, I know Vittorio would have done anything possible to help his friend. Rather, former friend. But if it was harmless, why was it coded in some ancient language almost no one could read? No, I didn't think helping them would be a good idea. I spat in her face, and earned another cut. I realized she was carving a pentagram into my arm. "Very original. Can't you think of something better than that?" Another cut. "Pain doesn't really bother me. I can take this all day." My voice held confidence, but I wasn't so sure about that. There was a lot of blood dripping down my arm.

"Very well then. Let's try another approach." She stood back a few feet from me, and I felt her power build.

A million knives stabbed my entire body, as I felt when we battled at The Chapel. The pain was worse this time as she took her anger and frustration out on me. I could not stop myself from crying out. Just when I thought I would faint from the pain, it stopped.

"Now will you help us?" She flipped the knife absently from one hand to the other.

Breathless from the pain, it took a few moments before I could respond. "Is that all you have?"

"What the hell is wrong with you, Elena? Just help her," Kevin said.

I wondered if he had endured the same from Elizabeth.

"You should listen to your little friend, you know."

"Why is that? You obviously can't finish a job. You didn't even complete your drawing on my arm."

"We'll get back to that soon enough." She thrust another burst of knife-wielding power at me, tearing screams from my throat. "You're not so strong when you can't defend yourself, are you?"

"I think I'm doing just fine," I panted.

"Maybe Neal's specialty will be a little more persuasive." I looked at Kevin's broken arm. "No, that wasn't from Neal. I did that when he called me a whore. Sometimes the use of your hands is the most satisfying." She cracked her knuckles.

Elizabeth did that? Now I was scared of her. If she was strong enough to break someone's arm, what else could she do to the human body?

"Oh, Neal," she called in a sing-song voice. "I think Elena would like to talk to you."

Neal walked into the room playing with a metal lighter, flipping the lid open and shut with a flick of his wrist. My pulse raced. I swallowed hard and scooted the chair back until it hit the wall.

"Looks like we may have found what frightens Elena. Neal, why don't you show her just what she has to fear?"

Neal held the flame near the arm that only had one cut, first just close enough for me to feel the warmth of the flame, then slowly moving it closer, until it burned my skin. I resisted as long as I could, but was forced to cry out. When I did, he stopped.

The horror of a camping trip when I was young surged to my memory. A spark from the dying campfire landed on my sleeping bag in which I'd slept, leaving second-degree burns on my legs. I had been afraid of open flames ever since.

Again he brought the lighter close to my arm, burning me in another place. I screamed, but this time he didn't pull the flame away. The smell of my burning flesh sickened me. The pain threatened to make me pass out.

"Stop it! Leave her alone!" Kevin shouted. This only angered Neal. He pulled the flame away and I felt his power grow. If his power was what I thought it would be, I wasn't sure I could handle it. The flames jumped down my throat, and I screamed until my throat felt raw. My body was engulfed in flames. The flames consumed my hair, shriveling it like burnt plastic. My skin blistered and blackened before becoming like leather. Still, I was alive, though I prayed for death. Even through this pain, I would never help them.

Then, I felt a familiar wave of power, and the burning stopped. I inspected my body best as I could while tied to the chair, saw my hair was still on my head, and my skin was not melted. I should have known. Tears poured down my face. Another minute and I think my mind would have broken. I wasn't entirely sure it was still intact.

I felt arms around me, and opened my eyes to find Vittorio holding me. His power enfolded me, easing my fear. I felt sane again. He started to pull the amulet from around my neck.

"Wait!"

"I must take this off you if you are going to be able to defend yourself."

"Not yet. I'm in so much pain and so angry and weak, I don't think I can control my power right now. If you take it off now, I don't know if I'll be able to focus it. I'm afraid I'll hit everyone around me, including you and Kevin. Please, get him out of here and untie me. I'll take it off once you're out of the room."

Before he could respond, and invisible force pulled him away from me. Samuel. Vittorio must still be weakened by the tranquilizer they gave him. I looked around frantically for Elizabeth and Neal. They were motionless heaps on the floor. At first I thought they were dead, then saw their chests barely rise and fall. At least they were out of the picture for now. Now, it was Samuel's turn.

CHAPTER FORTY-TWO

Vittorio and Samuel fought, though from an outsider's view they simply stood staring at each other. Their cries of pain seemed out of place if one didn't know what was going on. I was afraid Vittorio would lose the fight.

When Samuel's next attack subsided, Vittorio thrust as much power as he could at him. It threw Samuel against a wall, where he hit his head and was left unconscious.

"He will not be out for long. We have to hurry." Vittorio found Elizabeth's knife near my feet and cut me free, then went to Kevin.

"Get Kevin out first. He won't be able to fight with his arm, and has no defense against their power. I'll be right behind you."

Vittorio helped Kevin stand.

I realized we were in the middle of nowhere with no car. How would we get out of here?

A quick search of Samuel's pockets gave me his keys. I handed them to Vittorio. "Start the car. I'll be out soon."

"Be careful, mio amore. Please hurry." One short glance told me he did not want to leave me, but knew he must.

Elizabeth stirred on the ground.

"Go!" I shouted.

They ran as quickly as they could with Kevin in such bad shape. Elizabeth pushed herself to her knees, and then started to stand. I hoped Vittorio and Kevin were a safe enough distance away. I had no idea what my power would do now. I took the amulet off and shoved it in my pocket. It might come in handy later. The instant it was gone from my neck my power flared to life; anger not a strong enough word to describe it. It ripped through the room, devastating every living thing in its path. The magnitude of my power was physically staggering, but I had to get out of there.

Elizabeth clutched her head and let out a primal shriek unlike anything I ever heard. Neal was still unconscious, so I had no idea what my power did to him.

Running from the room, I left Elizabeth writhing on the ground in pain, relieved she was still alive. I didn't want to be responsible for anyone's death.

I reached the top of the stairs, and then made sure no one was following me. When I was certain I was alone, I tried to call my power back to me. It fought, still longing to damage those who had hurt me. I didn't have time for this. I finally put the amulet back around my neck, which forced my power back to me. It felt like it was tearing holes through my body, angry at being called back without completing its job. I screamed in pain.

Then, it all stopped.

Leaning on a table was all that kept me upright, and then I saw Samuel at the top of the stairs. I stumbled for the front door, weak and weary, and then dove into Samuel's Range Rover. "Drive!" I shouted.

Vittorio floored the gas pedal, tires spinning on the gravel driveway. I pressed the automatic lock button as Samuel ran out the front door. Finally, the tires caught, and we tore down the driveway. Vittorio focused on the road, for which I was thankful. He hadn't realized the full extent of my injuries, and I wanted us to be far away, someplace safe, before he could worry about me.

"Kevin, can you get your shirt off? I need to wrap something around my arm."

He struggled, but eventually managed to squirm out of it and handed it to me. I wrapped it tightly around the arm Elizabeth had paid the most attention to just as Vittorio turned to look at me. "I'll be fine, just concentrate on getting us someplace safe." Already the shirt was soaked with blood.

"You do not look fine, mio amore. You and Kevin need a doctor."

"I don't want to go to the hospital if we can avoid it. Too many questions to answer." My head swam from blood loss, though I tried to hide it from Vittorio.

"I agree," Vittorio said.

We thought for a few minutes, and then Vittorio sighed.

"I will call Dr. Fondazione. I have not talked to him in years, but hopefully he will help."

"Why haven't you talked to him?"

"We had a falling out when I started working for Porter Industries. He did not like Samuel and tried to tell me there was something malicious about him, but I would not listen. I suppose now he can tell me 'I told you so.' I hope his number has not changed."

Vittorio's hands shook as he put on an earpiece and dialed a number on his phone.

I wondered what Samuel had done to him. That would have to wait though.

"Julian. Please do not hang up. This is Vittorio. I know it has been long since we spoke, and we did not end our last conversation on the best of terms, but I desperately need your help. I do not know who else to turn to." There was silence on Vittorio's end, then he explained briefly what happened. "Yes, you were right. I am sorry. Please, will you help us? I will tell you more when we get there if you agree." More silence. "Thank you so much, my old friend. I am forever in your debt."

"He's going to help us?"

"Yes. He was not entirely pleased to hear from me, but as a doctor, he cannot turn down someone in need. He will meet us at his office."

I glanced at Kevin, who appeared to be sleeping. "I hope

Kevin will be alright. He's never been much of a fighter, but don't tell him I said so."

"I am most worried about you, mio amore." He glanced at the arm not wrapped up, at the burn marks. "How are you?"

"Not thinking about it. I can't think about it right now. Please."

"I am sorry. I hope you will be able to talk to me about it later."

"Later, yes, but not now. I can't handle it right now. Whose house was that?"

"It is Samuel's father's. He couldn't stand to stay there when Samuel's mother died, so he moved, but never sold it."

"What did Samuel want from you?"

Vittorio told me the same thing Elizabeth had.

"But why wouldn't he just ask us?"

"Nothing good ever comes of spells hidden in the ancient language. He would have known I would not willingly help him, or in this case, help you to help him."

"I had a feeling it was something like that. But how does he even know I can read it? What if I can't?"

"Samuel must be desperate. I do not know what would cause him to go to these lengths."

"That's not very comforting," I said.

"I am sorry, mio amore. It seems I have gotten you into yet another dangerous mess."

CHAPTER FORTY-THREE

We drove in silence until I remembered my phone call from Ms. Carmen. I told Vittorio about the map.

"I remember when Samuel tried to buy that map, now that you bring it up. And you say Courtney is missing again?"

I nodded. "Oh shit, you don't think Samuel has done anything to her, do you?"

"Hours ago, I would have said no. But now, I am not sure what he is capable of. We must find her."

"But how? If she's with Samuel, I doubt he'll let us near her. And she's not answering her cell phone."

"We will think of something. Does Ms. Carmen have a copy of this map?"

"I can call her and ask." A quick phone call told me that she did have a copy, and would slide a duplicate under the door to my office. That was a good thing; she didn't need to see us in the condition we were in.

More than an hour later, we made it to Dr. Fondazione's office without incident. It was an old, renovated building in the Central West End, a high rent district of town. He must do well in his practice. When we got inside, tension seeped out of my body. We were safe, for now. That's when it all hit me. I started crying and Julian wanted to give me a mild sedative, but I refused, insisting he take care of Kevin first.

Vittorio and I waited in another room. Only then did he notice I still wore the amulet. I had forgotten about it as well.

"I couldn't bring my power back under control." I told him

what happened when I took the amulet off. "I think it's safest if I leave it on until I am a bit stronger."

"I agree, mio amore. You seem to be on the verge of an emotional breakdown. Can you talk to me now?"

"Yes, now that all we have to do is wait for the doctor, I think it's okay if I lose it." I told him about the camping incident. "I've had a terrible fear of open flames ever since, so when Neal started burning my arm, I couldn't handle it. Then he unleashed his power on me. If you hadn't come when you did, I don't think my mind would have survived. If you hadn't..." I trailed off, sobbing, scared of the thought.

"You are safe now, mio amore." He held me while I cried, and his warm, soothing power embraced me.

Kevin cried out in pain.

I ran to his room across the hall. Julian had just set his broken arm. I sighed, relieved it was only that.

"What else did they do to you, Kevin?" Julian asked.

"I don't know. I'm embarrassed to say that all this," he motioned to his battered face, "is from Elizabeth. She and Neal used that power crap on me. I don't know what they did, just that it hurt. A lot. I think I passed out."

"Kevin, I need to use my power to try to find out what they did to you. We need to know if they did any damage to your mind. Are you okay with this?" Julian asked.

"I guess so."

"Try to relax. I promise I will not hurt you."

Julian's gentle, healing power wrapped itself around Kevin, bleeding off throughout the room. After a few minutes it dissolved into the air. "You will be fine. Your physical injuries are the worst of it. You might have nightmares about your ordeal, but they did no lasting damage."

"Thank god," I said. "Kevin, I'm so sorry. Can you ever forgive me?"

"It's not your fault." He tried to shrug, and groaned.

"Yes, it is. If you weren't my friend, this wouldn't have happened to you."

"I'm not blaming you. I'm gonna go to sleep now. The nice doctor gave me some medicine," Kevin slurred as he lay down on the examining table, and then fell asleep.

"Do you have a blanket to cover him with?" I asked.

Julian retrieved one from a closet. "Alright, let's go across the hall and have a look at you now, Elena."

He started by unwrapping the T-shirt from my arm, which had started to dry and stuck to my skin painfully. He soaked it in warm water to loosen it.

Vittorio gasped when he saw the extent of the damage. "Elena, why did you not tell me you were so badly injured?"

"I wanted you to get us here safely. You would have worried too much to focus on driving." I hissed as Julian pulled the cloth from my arm.

"You have lost a lot of blood, Elena. Do you know your blood type?"

"O negative."

"I'm going to give you a transfusion after we fix you up. I am surprised you are still walking on your own." Wide eyes belied the calm in his voice.

"I can be damn stubborn when I need to be."

He cleaned both my arms, and decided to start with the stitches in the worse one. I gritted my teeth as Julian sewed up my arm, but his needle was nothing compared to what Elizabeth had done to me, and I preferred to deal with the pain over the nausea anesthesia would have caused. When he finished stitching the partial pentagram, he moved to my other arm. Then, he examined the burns. He said they were third degree, put some burn cream on them, and wrapped my arm in gauze. "You'll have to apply this cream every four hours, and put clean gauze on each time. If the gauze gets soaked in pus, change it more often. It is important you keep the wounds clean.

"Now, I would like to examine your mind, if you agree."

"Okay." I was pretty sure my mind was at least partially damaged from Neal's attentions, and didn't think he'd be able to tell me anything I didn't already know.

He rested his hands lightly on either side of my head, and his power embraced me gently. I felt calm and soothed, as if everything was right in the world. I relaxed into that power, let him probe my mind, unconcerned with what he would find. I was sad when he pulled his power back to him.

"It seems you have been mildly traumatized by Neal's power."

I again explained the campfire incident.

"That makes sense. If you like, I can work with you over time to erase that fear from your mind."

"That would be great. It might have to wait, though. We have more important things to worry about right now."

"Just let me know when you are ready." Julian left Vittorio and me alone.

"Try to get some sleep, mio amore. I would like to talk to Julian for a while, and you need to rest."

"But what about you? What did Samuel do to you?"

"I will be fine. I will explain later. But for now, please try to rest. Will you do that for me?"

I nodded.

"Thank you. I am glad you are not more severely injured, though I do regret what they did to you."

"I'll be fine, Vittorio."

"I know. You are very strong, and very brave." We held onto each other for a long time.

"Rest now, mio amore."

CHAPTER FORTY-FOUR

When I woke, I walked across the hall to the room Kevin was in and found him still sleeping. Vittorio's and Julian's voices echoed down the hall. I did not want to interrupt, so sat in Kevin's room, waiting for him to wake.

When he did, I wanted to hug him, but restrained myself, not wanting to hurt him.

He stood and hugged me instead.

"I'm so glad you're okay, Kevin. I was so worried about you. When I saw you in that chair, I almost lost my mind."

"Calm down, Elena. I'll be fine. It's not like I haven't had a broken bone before." He sat back down and fumbled with his good arm to pull the blanket around his shoulders.

"You might want to take some time off work and get out of town for a while. I don't want you to get caught up in this again." I remained standing, hoping I could intimidate him into leaving.

"Fat chance of that. You think I'm leaving you alone in the middle of all this?" He continued fumbling with the blanket.

"I wouldn't be alone. Vittorio will be with me." I helped wrap the blanket around him.

"You know what I mean. I'm not leaving you. I may not be much help against those wackos, but I'll do whatever I can to help protect you."

"Thanks, Kevin." I sat down.

"What are you going to do now? You can't go back home since they know where you live."

"We haven't talked about it yet. I guess we can book a couple hotel rooms."

"A couple?"

"I'm not letting you go back home, either, not until this is over with."

"Just get a place with a hot tub, okay? And a gym would be nice."

"What are you going to do with a broken arm?"

"Watch the girls without broken arms." Kevin grinned, and I knew he'd be okay.

"How are you, really, Elena?"

"Hanging in there. The fire thing really freaked me out, but I'll be okay. Julian said he can help me erase that fear from my mind. Once this is all over, I'm going to take him up on the offer."

Vittorio's power called to mine as he entered the room. I jumped up to greet him, feeling very clingy. Part of me hated it, but the other part was accepting, especially since he gave me the comfort I needed.

"Do you feel strong enough to try removing the amulet, mio amore?"

I nodded.

"I would like Kevin to be elsewhere, just in case you are unable to control your power. He has no defense against it, and is already weak. I think he will be alright if he just goes to the other end of the building."

Kevin happily agreed.

I took a deep breath and concentrated, then slowly lifted the amulet over my head. My power pushed at me, wanting to be free, but I was able to keep it under control. I handed the amulet to Vittorio. "I want to see what happens if I kiss you. Do you mind?"

"I never mind when you kiss me." Mischief glinted in his eyes.

"You know what I mean. I want to make sure I can control my power, and that's when I'm most likely to lose control."

"I understand, mio amore. No, I do not mind." He leaned down and gently kissed me.

My power pulsed, but it was nothing more than normal for when we kissed.

"Guess everything is back to normal then, huh? Whatever normal is."

Vittorio knew the manager at a nice hotel in downtown St. Louis. He could book rooms for us under fake names so Samuel couldn't track us down.

"We should leave Samuel's Range Rover in a parking lot somewhere," Vittorio said.

"But how will we get to the hotel?" I asked.

"I can follow you, then drive you the rest of the way once you dump the car," Julian said.

"Thank you very much, my friend. We really appreciate this. I am eternally in your debt."

CHAPTER FORTY-FIVE

"Oh my god!" I exclaimed the next morning when I went to the hotel bathroom to change the bandage on my arms.

Vittorio leapt from the bed. "What? Are you alright?"

I showed him my arm. The burns were almost completely healed, and the stitches itched in the fresh scar that had once been a deep laceration.

"This is truly amazing, mio amore. I have seen people heal quickly, but never overnight like this. Your power is very strong indeed. We are going to have to get those stitches out. Let me see your other arm, then I will call Julian."

I unwrapped the gauze from my other arm to find it was healed just as completely. I sat on the bathroom sink.

"Mio amore?"

"I'm fine, just kind of shocked. This should have taken weeks to heal. I'm still not used to all this power stuff."

He put an arm around my shoulder. "Let me help you to the bed." I was pretty sure I could make it myself, but if he wanted to be chivalrous, I wouldn't deny him.

A knock resounded on the door between the two rooms. Vittorio unlocked the door, and Kevin sat gingerly on the bed next to me.

"How are you?" I asked. A rainbow of colors covered his face. I guessed the rest of his body didn't look much better under his clothes.

"Sore. You?" He looked at my arms and jumped back. "Holy shit. How the hell…?"

"It's part of my power, it seems. I can heal myself."

"I see that. Why didn't you just do it yesterday?"

"I didn't know I could. I woke up this morning, and my arms were healed."

"Can you heal me?"

The possibility hadn't crossed my mind. I looked at Vittorio.

"It is possible, but only time will tell," he said.

"Can't you at least try?" Kevin asked me.

"I wouldn't even know where to begin. This just happened."

"That hardly seems fair." Kevin turned away from me, arms crossed over his chest.

I couldn't blame him. This was all my fault, and he was right; I should at least try.

"Vittorio, could you teach me how to heal Kevin?"

"Mio amore, I wish I could, but it is too dangerous right now. You are weak, and it is very possible you would do him more harm than good."

"Fine, whatever," Kevin said.

"Why don't I order some room service?" Vittorio said.

"Good idea. I'm starving. I can't believe how hungry I am. I usually don't eat breakfast at all, and as much as I ate last night, I should still be full."

"You healed a great deal of damage. It is only natural that you would be unusually hungry."

Vittorio called Julian as we waited for our food to arrive. "Is there another doctor you would trust to send over here? I do not want Samuel and his people to follow you in case they are watching your office. Samuel knows I have not spoken to you in over ten years, but they will also know we were in dire need of medical help." Vittorio nodded, and I assumed that meant Julian would send someone else to remove my stitches.

We ate in silence, and then Kevin said he was going to check out the pool and sit in the hot tub to relax his muscles.

A half hour later there was a knock on our door. Vittorio

looked through the peephole, and then opened it. A young man who looked fresh out of medical school stood in the doorway. "I'm Dr. Robertson. Jim. You can call me Jim." He smoothed his white lab coat and fidgeted with his tie.

"Please come in, Jim," Vittorio said, closing the door behind him. "Try to relax. I realize this must be a bit out of the ordinary for you."

"Yes, well." Jim cleared his throat. "Let me see your arm."

Vittorio chuckled. "Oh, it is not me who needs the stitches removed. Elena, show Dr. Robertson your arm."

I held my arms out and Jim gasped. I wondered if we could trust him. "Did you come straight from Julian's office?"

"No, he called me at home. Why?"

"Just curious," I said. The chance he had been followed was very slim.

It definitely hurt as he snipped the stitches and pulled them from my healed arms. I was relieved when he finished and left.

"Vittorio, will you tell me what Samuel did to you now?"

He sighed, sat on the bed, and pulled me to him, holding me tight. "Yes. I will tell you."

CHAPTER FORTY-SIX

"One of Samuel's talents is manipulating people's thoughts. He can't make them do things they don't want to, but he can plant images in one's mind so vivid the person will believe it is real. I trusted him completely, and there is nothing about me that he does not know. He knows my deepest fears, and how to use them against me. He knows what makes me angry.

"When I met him at The Chapel, he injected me with a sedative so I would not be able to effectively fight back. I do not know why they used the amulet on you and not me. It is a very powerful object, not easy to make. I suppose that shows us just how scared of you they are. In any case, I could not protect myself, and he was able to get deep into my mind and plant the most awful images of," he shuddered, and I tightened my arms around him. "Of things that were being done to you." He held me tight and stroked my hair, as if reassuring himself that I truly was safe. "I heard Kevin's screams, heard you screaming in my mind, but was not sure which were real and which were Samuel's manipulations. Finally, I heard you scream so primally I thought my heart would burst. It gave me enough rage to break free of Samuel long enough to get to you. I'm so sorry I couldn't reach you sooner, Elena." He gently stroked my forearm, absently tracing the fresh scars. "I am angry with myself for being so weak."

"It's not your fault, Vittorio. You got to me when I needed you. That's what matters." I cupped his face in my hands.

"But what if I had not reached you in time? What if Neal broke your mind?" Tears glistened in his eyes.

"Don't think about that. He didn't, and I'm fine. And you and Julian are talking again, so that's a good thing, right?"

"I would rather not speak to him than have you injured."

A tear fell on my arm. I looked up at Vittorio's anguished face. I knelt in front of him and held his face in my hands, wiped away his tears, and kissed him gently. "Vittorio, I'm right here with you. I'm fine. It's okay now."

He held me tight, still crying.

Part of me wondered what images Samuel had projected in his mind, but the other part never wanted to know what would be so awful as to break a man as strong as Vittorio. I gently pulled back so I could kiss him again. "Let me help you forget." I kissed the tears from his face, moved to his neck and collarbone. As I felt more tears fall on my cheeks, I returned to his face to kiss them away, then moved down his chest. I covered his entire body in kisses, always returning to his face when I felt more tears. Soon, he stopped crying, and I knew he had other thoughts on his mind.

When he tried to sit up to hold me, I pushed him gently down onto his back. I wanted to take care of him. I lowered myself onto him, and he cried out for me, his hands kneading my breasts. We moved as one, and our powers merged. I held the thought 'take his pain' gently in my mind as we made love, somehow knowing that was what I had to do to heal the damage Samuel had done. When I did, he looked at me in wonder for a moment, then we were pulled back to the physical. The thought stayed in my mind, tending to Vittorio's mind as my body tended to his body.

We finished in a rush of power, and I collapsed on top of Vittorio, exhausted physically and mentally. His arms draped across my back and we fell asleep before our powers even returned to our bodies.

I woke on my back to see Vittorio looking down at me, smiling.

"How do you feel, mio amore?"

"I'm not quite sure how to describe it. I'm tired, but energized.

I feel, I want to say a sense of accomplishment, but that's not right. I don't know. How are you?" I sat up.

"You healed me. You erased the images Samuel planted in my mind. I will no longer be haunted by them as he hoped I would. You are truly amazing, mio amore."

"I'm glad it worked. Somehow, I just knew what to do. I wasn't scared about doing it. It was the most natural thing in the world. Well, second most natural," I grinned.

"Oh? And what is the first?"

"Making love to you." I pulled him to me to kiss him.

We lay together kissing until we heard a knock on the door.

"Are you guys dressed?" Kevin called through the door of our adjoining rooms.

I groaned. "Kevin has the worst timing." Louder, I shouted, "Go away, Kevin."

"That is not very neighborly of you," Vittorio teased. "We should pull ourselves out of bed. The day is wasting away, and we have much to do." He turned toward the door. "Just a minute, Kevin. Elena did not mean it."

"Spoil sport," I pouted. He kissed me lightly on the lips, went to retrieve our robes from the bathroom, then let Kevin in.

"You should really warn someone if you're going to do that power crap. What do you think the other guests are thinking?"

"Most people cannot feel the power. You seem to be sensitive, even if you do not have your own power," Vittorio explained.

"Lucky me. What were you doing? Never mind, don't answer that. I'll come back later when you guys are decent." He went back to his room, slamming the door behind him.

"Don't mind him," I said. "He gets grumpy sometimes. I don't blame him. After all we've been through, I'm healed and he's still in a world of pain, and we're next door having sex. I'd be upset, too, if I were him."

"We should get cleaned up so we can start trying to figure out what is going on, and include Kevin."

"Yeah, you're right, though I'd love nothing more than to lie in bed naked with you all day. I'll get a shower first."

"You do not want to shower with me, mio amore?"

"I do, and that's the problem. If we shower together now, we'll never get anything accomplished. Well, nothing productive, anyway." I went into the bathroom. "Would you order some food, please? I'm hungry again."

"Of course, mio amore."

CHAPTER FORTY-SEVEN

I understood why I was so hungry, but it still surprised me. I ate bacon, eggs, oatmeal, biscuits and gravy, and hash browns, and only barely felt full. Vittorio finished long before me, so took door duty when we heard a knock.

Julian had brought Vittorio's laptop, and the copy of the map Ms. Carmen left at my office.

They spoke quietly while I mopped up the rest of the gravy with a piece of toast. Why they gave me biscuits and toast I don't know.

"Julian and I are going to talk in the hotel bar for a while. Will you be alright?"

"Of course. I should spend some time with Kevin."

I hugged him before he left, and whispered, "Can I tell Kevin about what Samuel did to you? I know he's going to ask, and I don't want to lie to him. I think he deserves to know."

"Yes, mio amore. I understand you and Kevin have no secrets. If ever I tell you something I do not want you to share with him, I will say so."

"Thank you." I looked into his eyes and smiled. "Do you have any idea how much I love you?"

He returned the smile. "Perhaps a little."

I went to Kevin's room, sat on the bed next to him, and grabbed the remote. I flipped through the channels, waiting for Kevin to ask what I knew he surely would.

"I'm sorry I'm being such a jerk, Elena. I'm just having a hard time with this. I mean, I know it's not your fault, or Vittorio's, really, but I really got the short stick in all this. Elizabeth and Neal messed you up pretty bad, but you healed yourself already. Vittorio seems fine. Looks like they didn't do anything to him. But me, I get the shit kicked out of me, my arm broken, my face looks like raw hamburger. You should have seen how people were staring at me when I was in the hot tub. Why didn't Vittorio get messed up too?"

"He did. Samuel screwed with his mind." I turned the TV off.

"You'd never know it."

"You might not, because you don't know him. Kevin, please believe me, he got messed up real bad." I repeated what Vittorio told me about Samuel's power. "That's what I was doing with my power earlier. I was healing his mind."

"I thought you didn't know if you could do that?"

"I didn't. We were making love, and I just knew what I had to do. And now that I know-"

"Are you kidding me? You heal him, but not me? What's the deal with that?" He stood and paced the room.

"If you'd let me finish my sentence-"

"I've known you a lot longer than pretty boy has, and I think I deserve to be treated a little better than this. Jesus, Elena, you were a bitch when you were whacked out on drugs and everything, but I could understand that. This, I don't get it. This is just cold."

"If you'd shut the hell up for a minute, I'd tell you that now I know how to use my power for healing, I can heal you, too. But now, I'm not so sure I want to."

We stared at each other and I felt my power prickle down my spine with my anger. I didn't want to hurt Kevin. I wanted to heal him. But I was angry.

I gave in first. "Kevin, I'm sorry. Do you want me to try to heal you?"

"Try?"

"Well I haven't done it on a physical wound on anyone else. You know this is all new to me, so please stop giving me such a rough time."

He sighed. "I'm sorry, too, Elena. You're right. We're both really stressed out. But yeah, if you could heal me, that would be awesome. This battered face kind of sucks, and my arm hurts like hell."

"Alright. When I healed myself, I didn't feel anything. I don't know what it will feel like for you. But I'll do what I can. Just try to relax. Lie on the bed. I'm going to meditate for a few minutes to calm my mind. I'll tell you before I do anything." I sat on the floor, counting my breaths. As my mind calmed, I saw how to heal Kevin.

"I'm going to kneel next to you on the bed and hold my hands over your body. Just relax." I called my power, held the thought 'heal his body' in my mind, and pictured Kevin whole and well. I moved my hands along his body, not quite touching him, and gently pushed my power into him. I moved slowly, waiting until I felt each area was completely healed before moving to the next. When I finally felt that he was healed, I called my power back to me and collapsed on the bed, exhausted.

"Elena? Elena? Are you okay?" Kevin sounded frantic.

"Yes, just tired. Need sleep, and food."

"What do you want first?"

"Don't care." The world went black.

CHAPTER FORTY-EIGHT

When I woke, it was dark. I wasn't sure if it was nighttime, or simply the drapes blocking out the sun. Vittorio sat at the little table in the corner, hunched over his laptop. Kevin sat on the other bed watching TV. I sat up and saw a cheeseburger and fries on the nightstand. My stomach growled, ordering me to eat. I took a bite to find it was cold.

Vittorio came to me when I moved. "Are you alright, mio amore?"

"Yeah, I'm fine. Just really tired."

"You have healed both Kevin and me in a matter of hours. That would be draining for the most experienced practitioner of the power. For someone as new as you, who did not know how to heal until today...I am surprised you are awake already. I would have thought you would sleep for at least a full day."

"Sorry the burger's cold, Elena," Kevin said. "You were out like a light, and I didn't know what you needed, so I ordered it as soon as I could. I can go ask them if they can heat it up or something."

I was already taking another bite, shaking my head. "Uh-uh," I said through a mouthful of food. "Need to eat."

"Very ladylike," Kevin said.

I shot him a Look, and then swallowed. "You should be nice to me. Didn't you have a broken arm a few hours ago?"

"Yeah, thanks for that. I really appreciate it."

"Anytime."

"Let's hope not. Just because you can heal me like that doesn't mean I want to go around breaking my arm every day."

I finished the burger, and then relaxed into Vittorio's arms. I was still exhausted, and realized I was shivering. "Why am I so cold?"

"Your body is depleted of energy." Now that I was done stuffing my face, the full force of the coldness hit me, and I couldn't stop shivering. "The bathtub is very shallow. I think I will take you down to the hot tub to help you warm up. Kevin, will you be alright here by yourself for a while?"

"Sure thing, boss." He again saluted.

"Would you like to sit in the hot tub for a while, mio amore?"

"Yeah, that would be good. I'm freezing." Vittorio helped me change into a swimsuit that he must have had Julian bring with the rest of our clothes and I put my robe on over it. I was shivering so violently Vittorio had to help me walk down the steps to the pool area. I stuck a toe into the hot tub and it felt as if it would burn, but once my skin grew accustomed to the heat, it felt heavenly. I sank down into the hot water with a contented sigh.

"You and Kevin seem to be getting along pretty well. Boss." I said, grinning.

"We had a man to man talk while you were sleeping. It seems that when you healed him, he also got a glimpse into your heart. He was able to see how happy I make you. He told me that anyone who could make you that happy was okay by him. I promised him I would take the best care of you I could."

"I'm glad you two are getting along."

"You really do need to be more careful with your power Elena. If you use too much energy, you could seriously harm yourself. Healing takes a lot out of a person. Most will not perform more than one major healing in a twenty-four hour time span. You are far more powerful than anyone I have heard of. You will be able to do great things, mio amore."

"I don't want to do great things. I just want this mess to be over with, and to be with you." I huddled closer to him in the water.

"I know. We will have to take things one day at a time. We can do nothing else."

I wasn't entirely sure what he meant by 'great things,' but I was too tired to worry about it just then. I just wanted to be normal. Some of this magic stuff was cool, but I wasn't sure it was worth the cost.

CHAPTER FORTY-NINE

Vittorio and I spent the next day poring over stories about the Fountain of Youth. We studied the map, but couldn't figure out how the spell was hidden in it or what it might mean.

"It is possible that only the original will show the spell. Because we are working with a copy, it may not show up."

"Or maybe I just can't translate it like Samuel hopes."

"That is possible. I think he is grasping at straws. Your power is very strong, but there is no reason for him to believe you are the one strega this century to have that particular power."

"Do you think Clavius knows what Samuel is doing?" I asked while we ate room service for dinner.

"I do not know. It is very possible he does not; he has been so grief-stricken. That may be why Samuel's plans are just now ramping up. Courtney's appearance may have kicked it off as well."

"They were using each other," I said.

Kevin and Vittorio raised eyebrows as if on queue.

"When she ran away from home and Miriam started bringing her around, Samuel would have seen her as an easy opportunity to get the map Ms. Carmen wouldn't sell to him. He would have thought a young girl like her would be flattered by an older man's attention, so he flirted with her and started dating her as a way to get to the map.

"What he didn't know was Courtney was using him as a way into the coven. She would have done anything he asked if she thought he would convince Clavius to let her join."

"How do you know this?" Vittorio asked.

"The second time I talked to her at The Chapel, I could tell by the way she looked at Samuel that she didn't love him. She didn't outright admit it, but she didn't deny it, either." I paused. "I'm going to try calling her again."

This time, she answered. "Courtney, it's Elena. Are you alright?"

"Yeah, I guess so, but something weird happened to me and I don't know who I can talk to."

"You can talk to me if you want to," I said.

"Can I meet you somewhere?" She sounded nothing like the confident girl she was at The Chapel.

I muted my phone and asked Vittorio, who agreed. After setting up a time and place, I hung up.

Vittorio arranged for a cab to pick us up in the hotel parking garage and to drop us off a few blocks away from the coffee shop where we were meeting Courtney.

"Isn't this a bit of overkill?" I asked. "Nobody knows where we are, right? They would have come for us by now if they did."

"You are probably right, but I can not be too careful with your safety, mio amore."

"Or your own," I said.

Courtney sat in the back of the coffee shop, staring blankly down at the empty table. She wore no makeup, and I got a hint of the girl next door from the photo her mother had given me. I ordered drinks for all of us, hoping plain coffee would be alright for Courtney. "What happened, Courtney?"

"You'll probably think I'm crazy," she said, blowing on the coffee.

"I doubt that. Please, you can trust me," I said while looking her straight in the eye.

"I don't know. It's just..." she paused, and I waited. "Well, Samuel convinced me to borrow my mom's map. I know how much that thing means to her, so I made him promise he'd just make a copy then give it back. All he gave was a blank piece of paper, though, as if he thought I was dumb enough not to check it before I left."

"Did you say anything to him?"

"Of course. He made a big show of checking the poster tube it was in, then said he'd brought the wrong one home from his office. It seemed strange to me."

I raised an eyebrow at Vittorio.

Ask if anyone was with Samuel when he returned the map, he said in my head, so I did.

"Yeah, some guy. I've seen him a few times. I think his name is Neal." She took a sip of coffee.

She will have to stay someplace else until we know what Samuel is up to. If what I suspect is true, she isn't safe. Perhaps I could get her a room at our hotel.

How on earth was I supposed to tell her that without freaking her out? *Well, let's explain all this to her before scaring the crap out of her, okay?*

"I'm going to tell you something that may sound unbelievable, but please try to keep an open mind," I said. "There are people in the world who have a power. You might call it magic, but we prefer to simply call it power. Everyone with power has different abilities. One of the abilities some people have is to cause people to see things in another manner from reality. It's called glamour. You seem to be able to see through it."

"I don't understand," Courtney said, hands shaking around her coffee cup.

"It seems as if you are blessed with power, Courtney," Vittorio said.

She sank down into her chair and said nothing for a full minute.

"Courtney, are you alright?" I asked.

"I don't know. This is all so strange," she said.

"I understand, Courtney. I just discovered my power about a month ago, and it was quite a shock. My discovery was a bit more blatant than yours."

"What do you mean?"

"It was a very personal experience. I'll tell you about it some other time, perhaps, but not right now." I took a deep breath and let it out slowly. "Courtney, look, I don't want to scare you, but Samuel's mixed up in some bad stuff right now. Just to be safe, I don't think you should stay at home for a few days."

"Is he going to hurt me? I didn't even get the map back from him." She sat up straight again, hands still shaking slightly.

"I won't lie to you; I don't know. I want you to be careful. We're actually doing the same thing right now. You can stay at the same hotel with us."

"But I can't afford it, and my mom's out of town, and I wouldn't want to ask her for money anyway."

"I will pay for your room," Vittorio said.

"Oh, no, I couldn't let you do that."

"Please, it is nothing. I am well able to afford it, and would prefer to see you safe, even if we are being overly cautious."

Courtney searched my face, as if asking me what she should do.

I nodded, hoping she'd agree.

"Well, if you're sure."

"Yes, it is no problem," Vittorio said. He did relax a little and let Courtney drive us back to the hotel so she would not have to leave her car parked on the street.

CHAPTER FIFTY

"Perhaps I should set up a meeting with Clavius," Vittorio said once we were back at the hotel and Courtney was safely in her room.

"But what if he does know what Samuel is doing?" Kevin asked.

"There is only one way for us to find out," Vittorio said.

"I don't want you to get hurt by these people again. I won't let you just give yourself up to this guy if he is part of it all," Kevin said.

"I'll be armed, and it's the only choice we have. We haven't figured anything out on our own, and we can't just sit in this hotel forever."

"At least let me go with you," Kevin said.

"Absolutely not. Look what happened last time. You have no defense against them. What if they killed you?" Tears pricked my eyes at the mere thought of losing Kevin.

"Elena is right," Vittorio said. "It would be safer if you stay here. I do not want her to be distracted with worry over you."

Kevin stood. "Fine. Whatever. I'm going to my room."

A tear slid down my face as he walked away.

Vittorio reached across the table to wipe it away.

"I am certain he understands, mio amore. It must be hard on him to be stuck here with us, hiding, yet unable to do anything to help."

"I know. I just hope our friendship can take it."

"It will. Kevin cares for you very much. He will not let this

186

destroy your friendship."

I tried to smile.

"Elena, I want to start teaching you more about witchcraft. Now, more than ever, with the strength of your power, you need to be able to decide if you would want to be Sacerdotessa or not."

"You said yourself you don't even want to be Sacerdote. Why should I want something you don't?"

"I explained to you the obligation I feel to my coven and why I would not refuse the title. If you were by my side, it would be more bearable. We could do great things together." He reached for my hand.

"I don't want to do great things, with or without you."

"Sometimes, the fates have things planned for us which we do not like, but must go along with even so. You would not be blessed with such power if there was not some purpose for it."

"Blessed? You call this a blessing?" I pulled my hand away from his.

"Some would, yes."

"I don't care about some. I care about you."

He paused, as if debating how to answer. "Yes, I call it a blessing. I know it is hard for you to understand. I have had power almost all my life; you only a short time. You do not understand. In time you will see it for the blessing it is. Look at what you did for Kevin, and for me. Would you give that up?"

"Of course not! I would never take back having been able to heal both of you. It's all just a bit overwhelming. Please, be patient with me."

"I understand, mio amore. Will you at least let me teach you? I will not push you one way or the other if the opportunity arises, but I want you to know my ways, even if you do not adopt them as your own."

"Yes. I want to learn. I need something in my life to center me. But I don't know if I believe in God, much less many gods."

"All you can do is learn. Time will help you discover what you believe."

"I'll do my best for you, Vittorio."

"Do your best for yourself, mio amore. Now, shall we retire? We both have a lot to think about."

"Clavius has agreed to meet us at the Eat Rite Diner. It's a few miles from here, but we can make the walk," Vittorio said the next day.

"I'm going to tell Kevin where we're going, and when we'll be back." I knocked on the door to Kevin's room. "Kevin, Vittorio and I need to go out for a few hours." I explained the situation to him. "If we don't make it back, call Jerry. If we're going to be late, I'll call."

"I still think this is a bad idea."

"We don't have much choice. We haven't figured anything out ourselves, and we don't have time to waste."

"Arguing with you isn't going to do any good, is it?"

I shook my head.

"Alright. Be careful." He sat down and turned on the TV.

Vittorio and I started walking to the restaurant.

"Mio amore, your power is bleeding off you. You must concentrate," he said after a few blocks.

"Sorry. What if Clavius does know what Samuel is doing? We could be walking into a trap."

"That is why we must shield so strongly. We must block out any power he may attempt to throw at us."

We seemed to have arrived early, so got a table in the back and ordered coffee. I thought about ordering an appetizer, but my stomach flip-flopped too much for me to consider eating.

Clavius slid into the booth across from us. He studied me as he had the first time we met, and I felt the weight of his gaze even more strongly. As I had before, I froze, unable to think or move. I recovered as soon as Clavius took his eyes off me to look at Vittorio, and made a mental note to be careful with him. He affected me as strongly as Vittorio did, but in a much less pleasant manner.

"Tell me what is going on between you and Samuel." Right to business.

Vittorio told him everything. "Samuel seems to feel that not only does Elena want to replace Elizabeth, but that I am going to try to usurp your position. Please believe me when I say that is the furthest thing from my mind. I take my position as La Guardia very seriously, as I am sure you know, and that would go against everything I believe."

"Yet you want to bring someone as powerful as Elena into the coven."

"I love her. I did not know she had power when I first met her, and I have no intentions of taking over anyone's power or position. I simply want to share all aspects of my life with the woman I love."

"I sense the truth of your words. Yet Samuel believes you are a threat." He gave the waitress his drink order.

"I am sorry for what he believes. I have tried to explain it to him, but he will not listen."

"He also tells me that you were not willing to help him with something he needed."

Vittorio went still. "And what was that?" he asked, voice neutral.

"I think you know what I speak of."

"You know how dangerous the ancient spells can be. I will not put the woman I love in danger, even for one I viewed as a brother."

"You say that in the past tense. What has happened so seriously between you and Samuel to change your view of him? I know how close you were."

"Perhaps he did not tell you the full circumstances of the manner in which he tried to obtain our help."

"He told me that he asked you and you declined."

"I see," Vittorio said. The waitress brought fresh coffee for us and a mug for Clavius.

"Is there more?" Clavius asked when the waitress left again.

"Elena, show Clavius your arms."

I pushed up my sleeves and laid my arms on the tabletop so he could see my fresh scars.

"My goddess." The horrified look on Clavius' face made me feel a tiny bit better about him. Even if he was involved in Samuel's plot, perhaps he was not such an evil person. "I am so sorry about this. But...those are old scars. What game are you playing?"

"They are very fresh. Elena has the power to heal. But that is not important right now. Do you know what Samuel wanted from us?" Vittorio asked.

Clavius did not answer.

"Do you know he recently stole a valuable item?"

Again, no answer.

"Usually, when people don't answer, it means they have something to hide. What are you hiding?" I asked.

"How dare you question me? You are not even in full control of your power, yet you deign to question the Sacerdote of a coven that you hope to join? You should show a little more respect. What Vittorio doesn't know, is I can easily remove him as La Guardia, and banish him from the coven."

"I only have my coven's best interests in mind. Have I not served you loyally?"

"You have, but Samuel has been loyal, as well. Samuel understands my need."

"What need is that?" Vittorio asked.

"The need of my wife!" Clavius shouted, pounding his fists on the table.

The few other patrons turned to stare, forks halfway to their mouths.

"I am sorry Aerin is gone," Vittorio said softly. "I understand your pain."

"How could you? Who have you ever lost that would let you understand my pain?"

"I thought I would lose Elena when Samuel kidnapped and tortured her."

"It is not the same. You do not understand."

"Perhaps not, but I can try to imagine."

"You cannot! Samuel understands."

"His mother," Vittorio stated.

"What does he believe this spell will do?" I looked around and realized all the other patrons had left. That struck me as odd, but I didn't have time to worry about it just then.

"He is only trying to obtain it for me. I believe it will give me eternal youth and unlimited power," Clavius said.

"And what are you going to do with that power?" I asked, tired of being ignored.

"Get my wife back." His voice cracked with painful emotions.

"You think there is a spell to bring people back to life?" I failed to keep the derision from my voice.

"It must! I cannot live without her!"

"You're putting an awful lot of stock into something you don't even know will work. No one knows if I can translate the text."

"You could try." Clavius started at me, tears glistening in his eyes.

"I will not put Elena's life in danger. Attempting to translate an ancient spell could kill her if she isn't gifted with the power."

"You say that as if you had a choice."

The air was thicker, harder to breathe. I tried to strengthen my shields against whatever Clavius was about to do. A blast of energy so powerful I never could have kept it out overtook me at that moment, and I lost consciousness.

CHAPTER FIFTY-ONE

I woke tied to a chair, hands tied behind my back, and thought, "Dear god, not again." It took a few minutes for the fuzziness to wear off, and when it did, I realized I was back in the basement of Samuel's father's house.

Vittorio was bound in the same position on the other side of the room. No one else was around.

"Vittorio," I whispered.

He didn't move, still unconscious. How was it that I recovered from the blast of power before he did? I looked down at my chest, and saw a power-blocking amulet similar to the one from the last time I was captive around my neck. Crap. Vittorio wore one, too. Double crap. We were defenseless. I wiggled my wrists, hoping to be able to loosen the rope. I kept trying, and eventually shifted the rope around so I could reach it with my fingers. I picked at it, not really thinking I would be able to loosen it, but determined to keep trying. What else was I going to do?

As I struggled with the rope, Vittorio moved. "Are you okay?" I asked.

"I think so," he said, voice unsteady. "How long have you been awake?"

"Ten minutes or so. I was worried when I woke and you were still out. How did I recover before you?"

"I do not know. It may be that your power is stronger than mine. But that is not to worry about now." He blinked a few time then looked around, realized where we were and that we both wore amulets. "This is not good."

"I'm trying to loosen the rope around my hands right now. I'm not getting anywhere though."

Heavy footsteps came toward us from the hallway.

I lay my head to one side and closed my eyes. Maybe if he thought we were still unconscious, he'd go away; whoever it was.

"You cannot fool me, my sweet, little angel," Clavius said.

I opened my eyes. "I'm not your angel."

"Oh, but I think you will be. I think you will be whatever I want you to be." His power burst through me again, coursing through my body so intensely that I thought I would explode into a million tiny pieces. I screamed.

"Stop! Leave her alone!" Vittorio shouted, struggling against his bonds.

"Oh, but she is so much more fun than you are. Do you not remember this?" Clavius asked, and then directed his power toward Vittorio.

Vittorio struggled against it, clenching his jaw.

"That is why you are no fun to play with. Elena's screams are much more fulfilling than your silent sufferings."

He thrust his power into me again.

I tried not to scream, but he only kept making it stronger. I was going to pass out again, but just before I lost touch with the world, he stopped and brought me back to send a gentle wave of soothing warmth through me. That was so much nicer. Euphoria overcame me. The feeling of peace, love, and acceptance was so wonderful, I would have done anything as long as Clavius never made it stop.

"See, my little angel, I am not so bad now, am I?" He pulled his power away.

"Don't stop," I whispered, appalled at myself.

"Elena, fight him!" Vittorio shouted. "Think of our love, of how much I love you. He deceives you."

"Just do one thing for me, and I will give you such pleasure as you have never dreamed."

"Please," I begged.

"Translate the spell."

"Don't listen to him, Elena."

The sound of my love's voice was all I needed to pull me away from Clavius' power. "I'll never help you." His power tore through me again. This time he didn't stop until I lost touch with the world again.

When I woke, I did not see Vittorio in the room. I needed to know where Clavius had taken him. I struggled madly with the rope again, desperate to free my hands. My fingertips became sore with the struggle, but screams renewed my determination. I had never heard Vittorio scream, but knew it had to be him. He was so strong, so stoic, and my stomach churned to imagine what Clavius must be doing to him to force him to cry out in agony.

My fingertips were raw and sore, but finally I got a little leeway with the rope. I kept working at it until it gave up its hold on my wrists. When I saw how raw my wrists were, I thought about healing them, but decided to save my energy for more important things. I could deal with rope burn.

Once my hands were free, untying the rest of me was easy. I removed the amulet and put it in my pocket. I peered down the hallway, then headed in the direction of Vittorio's screams. I doubt Clavius would have heard me over Vittorio's screams and the maniacal laughter anyway. That's when I realized Clavius wasn't alone. The other laughter was a woman's - probably Elizabeth.

I looked around the corner of a doorway to see a fully equipped exercise room. Vittorio's hands were tied to a pull-up bar mounted from the ceiling. His legs were tied to a rack that must have held hundreds of pounds of free weights so that he could not kick out at his captors. His face was battered; blood trickled down his arms, chest, and legs. I could not see exactly what they had done to him.

Clavius, Samuel, and Jonah sat while Elizabeth gave her

attentions to Vittorio. Neal was nowhere in sight.

"Now will you give up your little ingénue for me?" Elizabeth asked.

"Never." Vittorio struggled against the ropes.

"You will not be so strong when you watch us slowly kill her."

I covered my mouth to keep silent.

"You will not touch her."

"You are hardly in a position to make demands. Perhaps if I show you some of my talents, you will change your mind."

"I will never change my mind about you, Elizabeth."

"Is that so?" She fumbled at his waist, and while I could not see what she was doing, I could imagine. I hoped I was wrong, as rage coursed through my veins. I was proven right when she dropped to her knees in front of him.

It took all my willpower not to run to her and beat her to a pulp with my bare hands. I knew I could not subdue four of them, though, and had to bide my time. Vittorio's breath quickened, his chest heaved, rising and falling. Jealousy tore through me, and tears tickled the corner of my eye.

"What do you say, my love?"

He spat on her. "Never."

She returned her attention to him. His breathing again quickened. I saw him clench his jaw in an effort not to cry out. I turned away, unable to watch her bring him like that.

"What about now?" she purred.

"That is no way to convince a man to sleep with you, Elizabeth," Vittorio said, jaw clenched.

"All you have to do is say yes, and it will all be over."

"No."

Again, she returned to him, and he clenched his jaw. He screamed out again, taking in breath after ragged breath. She wasn't going to bring him.

I could imagine what she was doing, and the thought horrified me. I tasted bile in my throat and swallowed hard, taking deep breaths to calm myself. Just as I was about to jump up to stop her, she pulled away from him.

"You will never have me, Elizabeth." Vittorio sounded weak as he shuddered from the pain.

"In that case, neither shall she!" She drew a knife from a sheath at her belt.

I leapt to my feet as she aimed it as his heart, but she froze in place as I felt a wave of power.

"That's enough, Elizabeth," Clavius said in his commanding voice. "I want him alive. Now go sit. You are finished with him."

As she walked away, I saw the damage she had done to Vittorio. She had sliced his chest and arms with her knife, his manhood with her teeth. Reason fled; I had to heal him. I pushed my power to him, willing him to be healed and whole again. He relaxed, and I drew my power back just as Clavius turned toward me.

I had enough time to put my shields in place before Clavius' power lashed out at me. The force of it battered me, but did not break through. I did not know how I would fight all three of them, but had no choice. I backed across the room as I matched my power to Clavius'. Neither of us made any headway, and the others followed to help Clavius. I thought of what they had done to Kevin, of what Elizabeth had done to Vittorio, and let the image fill my mind, fill me with rage. I used that rage to send my power out in a wave of metaphysical force, pushing all four them away from me. I unleashed a second wave of power, knocking all but Clavius unconscious.

He was stunned, and I took those precious few minutes to untie Vittorio and pull the amulet off his neck. He collapsed to the ground, weak from loss of blood.

I couldn't focus on him, though, as Clavius came at me again. He thrust his power at me and again I felt as if I would explode, but I gathered my will and fought to retain consciousness.

Vittorio's power grew behind me, and joined mine against

Clavius. I was surprised to feel the strength of his power, considering what he had been through, but didn't take the time to wonder. I pushed my electric power at Clavius, willing him to collapse, and trying to keep out his exploding power at the same time. I saw movement to one side, but couldn't take the time to focus on it.

I should have. Jonah had regained consciousness, and focused his power at me. My body was engulfed in flames, and I panicked. I collapsed to the ground, curled into the fetal position as the pain engulfed me.

CHAPTER FIFTY-TWO

Again, I woke to feel my wrists and ankles restrained. This was rapidly growing old. This time, however, they had put gloves on my hands so I couldn't fiddle with the ropes. The amulet almost choked me. I could not see Vittorio, and shouted out for him. I was in shock from Jonah's power attack, frantic, panicked.

"Your precious love cannot help you, so shut your mouth, bitch," Elizabeth said, kicking me in the side. I cried, terrified of the fire. It was gone now, but my mind wouldn't believe that it wouldn't return. I knew I was in trouble, and though Jonah hadn't completely broken my mind yet, I felt on the verge of a panic attack. I needed Vittorio's comfort, and screamed.

"What are you screaming about?" Elizabeth asked as she kicked me again.

I shook my head back and forth and cried, my body shaking.

"Are you cold? Jonah could remedy that."

"No!" I screamed, terrified the fire would return. "Vittorio!"

"I told you, he can't help you. Samuel is having a chat with him." As she said that, I heard Vittorio call out my name. I remembered what Samuel had done to him before.

"Vittorio, I'm okay. Don't believe whatever Samuel is showing you," I called out. I was far from okay, but the lie seemed acceptable considering the consequences.

"Jonah, maybe you can make Clavius' little angel shut up, because she won't listen to me."

"No, no, no," I cried when I saw Jonah standing above me. His power was gentle at first, mere warmth over my body. Slowly, the heat grew until I thought my skin would melt. I tried to tell myself it wasn't real, but the fear of fire deeply embedded in my mind would not listen. He sent the heat in waves, backing off every few minutes so I wouldn't lose consciousness, laughing the whole time as I screamed.

"Stop!" I never thought I would be so happy to hear Clavius' voice in my life.

"We're just having some fun," Elizabeth whined.

"I said stop. I want her mind whole so she will fully understand what we are going to do to those she holds dear. Then we will decide her fate."

That didn't sound good, but I was too busy crying and shaking to grasp what he meant.

"You didn't break her already, did you, Jonah? I will be very unhappy if you did." Clavius probed at my mind with his power, and I shuddered. "Nothing I can't fix. But next time, be more careful." His power embraced me, comforting, taking away the fear in my mind.

I stopped crying, but still shook as my body tried helplessly to reject his power.

"Leave us."

Clavius knelt on the floor next to me and wrapped his arms around me in a gesture that would have been comforting had it come from Vittorio, but was disturbing from Clavius.

I tried in vain to move away.

"It's okay, my little angel. They won't hurt you anymore. I won't let them. You're mine now."

"I'll never be yours." I struggled weakly against his arms.

"Oh, you will be."

"I am Vittorio's."

"Vittorio will not live much longer. Then, you will most certainly be mine." He caressed my face, ran his hands over my body and kissed me.

"What about Aerin? What would she think of this?"

Clavius paused; his power lessened. "She would understand."

"She'd understand you molesting another woman?"

"I love her. I do not love you. And I believe you will make my power stronger, as you have Vittorio's."

Vittorio's power had become stronger because of me?

Clavius watched the thoughts cross my face. "He hasn't told you? How selfish of him. His power is noticeably stronger since he met you."

I couldn't risk thinking about that right now, so pushed it aside. "I would not be okay with Vittorio fucking another woman just to gain more power."

"And that is where you and Aerin differ. Not that you have much of anything in common with my sweet Aerin. But she understood that we must sometimes do unappealing things to strengthen our power. She and I accept that harsh reality."

I struggled uselessly against my bonds.

Clavius enjoyed every minute of my torture. "Ah, my little angel, in time you will not be so repulsed by me."

I screamed in wordless frustration.

"What did you do to her?" Vittorio growled as Samuel led him, still restrained, into the room.

"Nothing you have not already done."

"You bastard." Vittorio struggled to get to Clavius, but Samuel had too strong of a grip on him.

"Your little slut may have healed you once, but that just makes it more fun for us. We get to damage you all over again," Elizabeth purred.

"If you kill us, we won't be able to help you."

"Obviously, we won't kill you until we have what we need. And you will help us. You see, Samuel took Jonah's car and followed you to your dear doctor after you escaped. With a little persuasion, Julian told us where you were hiding. So while you so stupidly met me at the restaurant, Samuel went to your hotel and found your slut's friend. It seems we didn't scare him badly enough the last time."

"Leave him alone!" I shouted.

Jonah returned with Kevin, who had been beaten again. As much as I hated his involvement, though, I was relieved they hadn't found Courtney.

"Help us, and we will."

"Vittorio, please, we can't let them hurt Kevin anymore. We have to do what they want."

Vittorio nodded once, and sighed, clearly not happy with the decision, but he knew what Kevin meant to me. And he was too good of a person to let someone be tortured if he could stop it.

"I knew you'd see it my way," Clavius said.

CHAPTER FIFTY-THREE

Samuel led us upstairs to a room that must have once been a study. The bookshelves were empty now; I assumed the books had been moved to his father's new home. He pointed to some chairs around a coffee table, and we sat. Ms. Carmen's map had been laid on the table.

The others stayed in the basement, agreeing the fewer people with me the less distracted I'd be.

"I'm going to take your amulet off now, Elena. Don't try anything stupid or your friend will suffer for it."

"I won't," I said, heart racing. I didn't know how he expected me to concentrate on anything when Kevin was in danger, but I had to try.

My power fought to escape my control. Even though I didn't use it often, it was always free, and did not like being confined by the amulet. I managed to keep it in check, wishing I had full control. I realized I would never have full control of my power though; not entirely. While the power did belong to me, it was also its own entity, sharing my body.

"Focus on the map. Try to read it," Samuel instructed, as if I didn't already know what he wanted from me.

First, I only looked at the map, studying the markings on it. A small breath of magic emanated from it, but it was completely foreign. I couldn't decipher a thing.

After a few minutes, I held my hands above the map. I didn't want to touch it yet, afraid there might be some spell to harm if I did. I felt nothing malicious, so gently laid my hands on the surface.

My whole body tingled from the power in the ancient document. I jerked my hands away.

"What's wrong?" Samuel asked.

I told him what I'd felt.

"You can read it! I didn't feel anything from it," he said.

"That does not mean anything," Vittorio said. "It may only mean her power is stronger than yours."

Samuel glared at him, but said nothing.

Ignoring them, I picked up the map and tried to translate the strange markings on it.

"Try to relax, Elena. Meditate for a few minutes if you must. Perhaps it is like one of those magic eye posters where you have to look through the design to see the hidden image."

I tried holding the map in various positions, not holding it, turning it every which way, but came no closer to translating it after half an hour. "I can't do this alone. I need help," I told Samuel.

"What do you mean?" he asked.

I hesitated, knowing he wouldn't like what I was going to ask for. I didn't even know if it was possible, but my power whispered that it was.

"Well, what is it?"

"I think if I could try to join my power with Vittorio's, I might be able to read the map."

"Do you think I'm stupid? As soon as I take the amulet off him, you'll try to overpower me."

"Why would we do that?" I replied. "If we do, Clavius will kill Kevin, and that's exactly what I'm trying to avoid." I stared him right in the eye, unwavering.

Samuel pondered my request, and seemed to decide he could believe me. He untied Vittorio's hands and took his amulet off.

Vittorio reached for my hand, and we let our power loose, swirling together around us. I again picked up the map with my free hand and scanned it casually, trying not to concentrate too hard on it. After a few moments, the letters on the page seemed to swim and rearrange themselves.

"Do you see that?" I whispered.

"I see nothing, mio amore."

I watched the letters continue to move, hardly believing it was possible. They finally settled into a pattern I could read; they had changed to English.

"Give me a pen and paper," I told Samuel.

He did as I asked, and I wrote the spell down. Once I had, Samuel rushed to tie our hands again and put the amulets back around our necks, and then led us back to the basement.

CHAPTER FIFTY-FOUR

When we returned to the basement, I handed the piece of paper to Clavius. "What makes you think I won't use the spell on myself?" I asked.

"One must hold the map while chanting the spell in order for it to work. And I will never give you the map. In fact, I think I'll burn it when I'm done just to be sure you'll never get your hands on it." He turned to Vittorio. "Now that I will be more powerful than anyone, do you maintain that you do not want to overthrow me as Sacerdote?"

"I have seen your true nature. I love my coven and will not allow you to manipulate them. I will take your position," Vittorio said.

"Wrong answer. You must enjoy watching your love suffer."

He sent a wave of power through Kevin.

"Stop! We did as you asked. You promised you wouldn't hurt him."

"I never promised. I am not that stupid."

"Please, don't hurt him."

"We are just beginning, my little angel, unless Vittorio agrees to revoke his threat and offer his allegiance to me."

"Don't do it," Kevin moaned.

Elizabeth slashed him across the cheek with her knife.

"Please stop," I begged.

Vittorio said nothing.

Elizabeth's power flared, and Kevin cried out in pain. She followed up with a carefully placed stab that caused no major damage.

When she stopped, Kevin looked at Vittorio and said, "Don't give in to them. I'm not important."

"Yes, you are," I cried.

Elizabeth slashed his midsection.

"Vittorio, please. Kevin won't survive this much longer. Look how much he's bleeding."

"Alright, stop. You win," Vittorio said.

"Say you will follow my command."

"I will follow you." His shoulders slumped.

"And you will give me your little angel as Sacerdotessa."

"No!" he cried.

"Yes, he will. Just let Kevin live," I said.

Vittorio looked at me in horror.

"I can't watch them kill him. I'm sorry, my love, but I can't."

"Fine," Vittorio muttered.

"Swear it."

"I swear," he said, barely audible.

I couldn't stand the look of pain in Vittorio's eyes as he swore his allegiance to Clavius.

"Good. Now, Elizabeth, if you will do as we discussed?"

Elizabeth turned to walk away from Kevin, suggesting his torture was over. Then, she turned around and thrust her knife into Kevin's heart.

I don't know if Kevin's scream or mine was louder. I crawled to him and pressed myself to him in as much of an embrace as I could with my hands still bound behind my back.

He slung one arm around me.

"Kevin, please don't die. Please, Kevin. I'm so sorry. Don't leave me."

"Make him pay," he whispered.

"No, you're not going to die. Please, Kevin. You can't leave me." I tried to heal him, but the amulet was still around my neck, my hands still tied. I was helpless.

"Vittorio will take care of you. Kill Clavius for me." His arm slid from my shoulders and his body went slack.

I stared at Clavius through my tears. "You will pay for this, you bastard."

"Is that so? And what are you going to do, all tied up and powerless? Nothing. And now, you will see how strong I truly am." Samuel handed Clavius the map, carefully rolled up. He held the map in both hands and chanted the spell three times. Power rose in the room, threatening to suffocate. It was not Clavius' power; rather the foreign power of the ancient spell. The map glowed in Clavius' hands and I wondered if it would save him the trouble of burning it himself.

He seemed to grow younger. He turned and tested his power on Vittorio, who screamed in pain. I felt that Clavius power was stronger than before. I feared we would never be able to defeat him now, even if we could get free of the ropes and amulets.

"Such power! I will live forever. See how I will rule!" He projected his thoughts into our minds. He sat high upon an onyx throne. A woman I assumed was Aerin stood by his side. People who I sensed were the other coven members knelt at his feet, proclaiming their loyalty and everlasting love to Clavius. His thoughts said he would kill anyone who opposed him. And the first he would kill would be Samuel. Samuel was too powerful, too ambitious, too much of a threat.

I don't think he meant for that last part to reach us, and he didn't seem to notice. Samuel's face said he certainly had noticed. He moved closer to Vittorio and knelt down beside him when Clavius wasn't looking. I saw him whisper something. He stood just as Clavius turned to look at him.

"And you, Samuel, you will take the place of La Guardia. You have served me loyally, and I will soon need a replacement."

Vittorio scooted closer to me. I saw he had a knife and that his hands were free. He cut me free as well. "When Clavius is not looking, remove the amulet, but not before. We will have to be quick and stun him. I only hope the amulet will work on him now that he has used the spell."

"Come, Samuel, come and chant the spell with me. Be young and powerful," Clavius beckoned.

As Samuel walked toward Clavius, he reached behind his back and drew a gun that was tucked under his shirt. My gun. In one quick movement he shot Clavius in the heart. Clavius collapsed to the ground.

Jonah and Elizabeth battered Samuel with the full force of their power, overcome by rage and sorrow at the death of their Sacerdote.

Vittorio and I removed the amulets from our necks. "Should we help him?" I asked.

"He did help us." He tucked the amulets into his pocket.

"That's only because Clavius was going to kill him. Personally, I say let Elizabeth and Jonah do what they want with him."

"You are becoming coldhearted, mio amore." There was no sentiment to his words, just a statement of fact.

"Can you tell me you truly wish to help him after everything he did to us?"

"No, mio amore, I cannot."

I wondered what the hell we were going to do then when movement caught my attention. It was Clavius, standing unharmed.

CHAPTER FIFTY-FIVE

"Did you really think one little gunshot wound would kill me, Samuel? I was going to make your death fast and painless, but now I will enjoy making it slow and watching you suffer." He turned to Elizabeth and Jonah. "I am pleased to see your reactions. You make me very happy with your loyalty. Have some fun with Samuel. Do what you please with him, but leave him alive. I want to kill him myself."

I watched the gun leave Samuel's grasp and float through the air to Clavius. Telekinesis. Samuel had mentioned that some stregas had that power, but it was still unsettling to see in person.

"And you, Vittorio, you are proving to be stronger than I ever thought. I wanted to enjoy your slow, painful death, but it is clear to me I would be smart to end your life quickly, so you will no longer remain a threat to me. Then, I will have my way with your love, and take her power as my own."

I aimed the full force of my power at Clavius, dreadfully aware it would not be enough.

He laughed. "Oh, my little angel, you have heart, but you will never be able to win. Perhaps once you would have been a fair match, but now, no one will be able to defeat me. Watch, now, as I kill your love."

I felt Clavius' power gain strength, saw its icy blue color as he aimed it at Vittorio. The bleed-off caused me great pain, as well. I could only imagine how badly Vittorio suffered. I screamed in protest, helpless.

Without warning, the blast of power stopped. Vittorio was

curled in a ball on the ground. "What happened?"

Vittorio shook his head to indicate he didn't know.

Samuel stood behind Clavius, who was now on his knees.

I went to see what happened, scared I would feel another painful blast of power at any moment.

When I reached Clavius, I saw that Samuel had stabbed him in the back, through the map. A wound such as that shouldn't have been as damaging as it appeared to be. He writhed in pain.

I looked at Clavius and realized that he was, in fact, dying. His face contorted in pain, and he was screaming incoherently. I caught two words - it burns. I wondered if the map acted as a type of poison in his system.

When he stopped moving, I wanted to be sure he was truly dead this time. I checked his neck for a pulse, and felt nothing. Then, his body twitched. I tore the map out from under him and stabbed him in the heart through it with the knife Samuel had given Vittorio. No more twitching.

I had never killed anyone before. I concentrated on my breathing, and tried to push the shock to the back of my mind. Now was not the time for a breakdown. There were still other things to worry about.

As if to illustrate that point, my body was stabbed by a thousand knives. The full force of Elizabeth's power struck me, giving me no time to react and put my shields in place. I screamed. Where was Vittorio? Why wasn't he helping me?

The pain stopped. I slammed my shields in place tighter than ever. I looked to Elizabeth, and found her in a power struggle with Samuel. That left Jonah free to focus on me. I thrust electricity into his body before he could act, moving closer to him as I did. When I was close enough, and he was on his knees on the ground, I put the amulet around his neck. I did not stop the flow of my power. I had to find some way to restrain him. Where were those ropes when I needed them?

I forced his hands behind his back, focusing my power on him the entire time so he wouldn't fight back. The rope that had bound Vittorio and me was too short since we'd cut through it. Thankfully, I found a roll of duct tape sitting on top of a toolbox in the corner, and bound Jonah's hands and feet, then found the straps they had used to keep us in the chairs. Hoping Jonah was secure enough, I took the duct tape with me, hoping for the opportunity to restrain Elizabeth and Samuel.

Samuel was winning their fight. Elizabeth was on the ground, rocking back and forth, muttering, "No, no, no," over and over again. I didn't want to imagine what horrible images Samuel projected into her mind to make her shake like she was. I saw the amulet that had been around Vittorio's neck on the ground next to him. I also saw that Vittorio was not moving. I had to make sure we were safe before I could help him, so I grabbed the amulet. Samuel's attention was focused on Elizabeth, so I snuck up behind him, draped the amulet around his neck, and forced his hands behind his back before he could react. He was much stronger than me, and my power did not faze him like it had Jonah. I couldn't let him break free and remove the amulet. I had to go for a low blow. I reached my leg between his and kneed him in the groin. He fell to his knees, giving me the opportunity to bind his hands.

I still needed to restrain his feet, and he was able to get away from me before I could. He got to his feet and kicked me. Fortunately, it sent him off balance and he fell again. I kicked him in the side, and much as I hated it, the head. I never was a fighter, but my life was on the line. The kick to the head dazed him enough for me to tie his feet together. I was as safe as I was going to get from him.

I didn't know what to do about Elizabeth. There were no more amulets, no way to restrain her power. I looked to her, still rocking back and forth on the ground, knees pulled to her chest. It appeared as if Samuel had done significant damage to her mind. I would have to settle for tying her up, and hope it was enough.

When I was finally satisfied our enemies were restrained, I ran to Vittorio, who still was not moving. I did not see his chest rise with breath. I felt for a pulse, finding nothing.

CHAPTER FIFTY-SIX

I screamed in anguish, wishing I were dead, too. How could I live without Vittorio? I pulled him into my lap, holding him. He was still warm, his skin still soft to the touch. I rocked back and forth with him in my lap like mother rocks a child who has had a nightmare, only this nightmare was real. Vittorio was dead. A voice in my head reminded me that Kevin, too, was dead, and I was alone. Madness crept through the corners of my mind. Samuel had stolen Elizabeth's sanity; Clavius had stolen mine.

I don't know how long I rocked Vittorio in my arms. Something tugged at my power. I ignored it, not caring if any of the others had broken free. Let them kill me. I didn't even care if Clavius rose from the dead. Any torture they could inflict on me could not be as bad as the pain of losing Vittorio.

My power pushed against my body, trying to get out. I pushed it down, but it fought me. I was too weak to fight it, and let it go. I didn't care what it did. It pushed gently out of my body toward Vittorio. Was my power mourning, as well? It flared up for a moment, as if trying to tell me something, and pushed toward Vittorio again. I held him close to me, unsure what my power was trying to tell me, too bereft to care.

The slightest breeze tickled my neck where Vittorio's head rested. I almost didn't notice it. Again, I felt the breeze. It was warm. The third time, I realized it wasn't a breeze at all, but Vittorio's breath. He was alive! That's what my power was trying to tell me. I tried to pull myself together so I could concentrate. I whispered a prayer, "Goddess, please let him live. Please do not take him from me," and let my power embrace Vittorio. I held the thought, "Heal him," in my mind as I let my power surround him, flow into him and through him. At first, nothing happened. I feared it was too late. Then, the breath on my neck grew stronger. I maintained the flow of my power through his body, willing him to live.

Time passed, and I grew weak. I didn't know how much energy I had left. If it took every last drop of me, I would keep trying until I collapsed. Finally, Vittorio moved. He raised his head from my shoulder and said, "You can stop now," so softly I almost didn't hear him. He was weak, oh so weak; I didn't want to stop. I wanted to heal him. I continued to let my power flow through him. He pulled away from me and said, "Stop, mio amore, please, you will hurt yourself if you do not." I didn't want to listen, wanted to heal him, but he was alive, and I was weak, so I called my power back to me. It returned, sluggish. Vittorio and I held each other, both of us drained.

"Mio amore, you have done the impossible. You brought me back from death."

"What?"

"I was dead. I felt my life force leave my body. I saw the Goddess. How did you do it?"

I tried to explain.

"Your power acted on its own. That is amazing."

I was too drained to think about the meaning of that. I didn't understand, and didn't care. "Can we save this for later? I can barely sit up I'm so tired."

"Yes, mio amore, we both need rest. But we may not get it quite yet." He looked to our captives, and I was relieved to see they were still restrained.

CHAPTER FIFTY-SEVEN

"What are we going to do about them?" I asked.

"I do not know yet. But before we discuss anything, I must try to reach Julian."

I held my breath, praying Julian was alright. I had a sick feeling in my stomach, as if I was forgetting something very important.

"Julian? Julian, are you alright?" Vittorio asked. After a moment, his shoulders relaxed, and I let out my breath. "Thank goddess. I cannot talk long, but will call as soon as I can. I am so sorry to have involved you in this." After a few more moments, he said goodbye then hung up.

"We must figure out what to do here." He looked at my face. "You have an idea, mio amore?"

"Yes. I don't know if you'll like it or not. I know this is all supposed to be secret, but I really don't know what else we can do with Kevin and Clavius' bodies here." I paused, afraid of what he would think. "I'd like to call Jerry and ask him to help us."

"Jerry is your police officer friend?" Vittorio's face and voice were neutral.

"Yes."

"But you said you have not spoken to him in nearly three years."

"That's true, but I still trust him. Police are going to get involved, and I'd rather have him be the first to arrive. If you have a better idea, if you know who we can trust in the coven, tell me."

Vittorio stared past me.

I turned to see what caught his attention, but nothing was

there.

He continued to stare. "You are right. I do not know whom we can trust, and we need help. I do not want to involve Julian in this anymore, even if he could do something without risking his career. Yet it goes against everything I have been taught to tell an outsider of our power. What will he say to it?"

"I don't know. I'm sure it will be hard for him to believe. I had a hard time with it, and I have power. But Kevin accepted it."

"Are Kevin and Jerry alike?"

"Not really, but Jerry was like a father to me until we quit speaking. I don't think he'll just dismiss me as a nutcase."

"I hope not," Vittorio said softly.

"I didn't mean he'd have us committed." How could I have been so thoughtless to say something like after Vittorio's childhood experience?

"It is alright, mio amore. I know you did not mean it like that. But that is a very real possibility."

"I don't think we have to worry about Jerry. It will be hard for him to accept, but I think he will, eventually. And I don't know who else we can turn to."

Vittorio was silent for a long while. "Very well. Call your Jerry, see if he will help us. But be very careful how you present this to him. If nothing else, we have two dead bodies here. We could be arrested as suspects."

"Thank you, Vittorio."

I hoped Jerry hadn't changed his phone number since we last spoke. After three rings, someone picked up the phone. I held my breath. "Jerry?"

"Who is this?"

I recognized his gruff voice. "Jerry, it's Elena." I paused, waiting for him to say something. "Don't hang up, please. I need your help."

"You aren't on drugs again, are you?"

"No! Jesus, Jerry, no. I'm still clean." That was why we fought when I quit the force. He was afraid I'd stop taking Zoloft and go back to illegal drugs. Nothing I said would convince him otherwise, and my therapist convinced me it would be healthier for me to end my relationship with him, at least for a while.

"Well, what's wrong?"

"It's really hard to explain, and I hope you believe me. I need you to keep this to yourself until I see you. Please, you can't tell anyone."

"Tell anyone what?"

"Can you meet me out in Wildwood?"

"Do you know what time it is, Elena?"

"Actually, I have no idea. I've had a really tough couple of days, and I don't know who else to turn to." I gave Jerry the address. "Please, will you meet me there?"

"Three fucking years and you drag me out of bed in the middle of the night. Alright, fine, I'll meet you there."

"Come alone. And promise not to tell anyone?"

"Goddammit. I always had a soft spot for you. Never understood why, you're nothing but trouble." He sighed, and I pictured him rubbing his face with his hand. "Alright, I promise."

"Thank you, Jerry. Thank you so much. You have no idea what this means to me."

When Jerry arrived, I was grateful to see two cups of gas station coffee in his hands. I spent the next hour trying to explain everything to him. He didn't believe it, and I knew I'd have to prove the magic bit to him. "What aren't you telling me, Elena? And don't say 'nothing.' I hear it in your voice."

"Remember Kevin?"

"Sure. Why the hell you didn't listen to him sooner, I'll never understand. I always liked that kid. How is he?"

A sob escaped my throat. "He's dead."

Jerry choked on his coffee. "Shit. What happened?"

I told Jerry everything about the night.

"You have two dead bodies, one of which you admit to killing yourself?"

"I swear it was self-defense." I wiped the tears from my face.

"I believe you, Elena, but I can't keep this quiet." He took a sip of coffee, trying to process everything I'd told him.

"I know, and I never expected you to. But I wanted you to be the first person here."

"What do you think I can do?"

"I don't know. Isn't there some way you can get involved?"

"Lucky for you I don't work for the city anymore. I'm a state trooper. Technically, since you're in unincorporated Wildwood, yeah, I can be involved."

"Oh, thank you, Jerry. I'll just feel better knowing you're there."

CHAPTER FIFTY-EIGHT

I went over everything with Jerry again, this time while he took notes.

"You're telling me Samuel has some kind of power to break people's minds?"

"No, he can project images into someone's mind, and they don't know if it's really happening or not. Whatever it was he showed Elizabeth was so horrible her mind snapped. I understand the feeling. Jonah almost broke me when he made me feel like I was consumed by fire."

"I don't believe it. Elena, please tell me the truth. If I think you're obstructing justice with this cockamamie story, I'm going to have to have you arrested."

I decided it was time to show him. I tried the light orb trick I used with Kevin. "Nice trick, but you could do that with a flashlight."

"Search me. I don't have a flashlight."

He did. "I still don't believe you. It could be some sort of optical illusion."

I rolled up my sleeves and showed Jerry my scars.

His eyes widened. "What the hell happened to you?"

"These are only a few days old. I have the power to heal."

"I haven't seen you in three years. Those could be old."

"Fine. Give me a knife." I knew I shouldn't do this after all the power I'd expended on Vittorio, but it was the only way.

"Excuse me?"

"Please, Jerry, I'm trying to make you believe me. Give me a knife. I'm not going to stab you. I'm on your side, remember?"

"I'm not so sure about that now that you're making up stories."

"I promise I'm not going to stab you." Jerry reluctantly handed me a small pocketknife. I pushed up my sleeve and drew the knife across my arm, nice and deep.

Jerry drew in a sharp breath.

I called my power while he watched the wound heal in moments, mouth open. "Now do you believe me?" I let Jerry inspect my arm.

"I don't see how it can be a trick. I guess I have to, but -" For once, Jerry was speechless.

I collapsed into a chair and let him recover. I understood why it was such a shock.

"What else can you do?" Jerry finally asked.

I explained about the electricity. He insisted I show him, so I did, as gently as I could, and for only a second. I then explained that I was still learning how to control it.

"Why are you telling me this?" Jerry's eyes were wide.

"Nothing that has happened would make sense without it."

"What about your boyfriend?"

Vittorio was in the next room so Jerry and I could have some privacy while we talked.

"What about him?"

"What can he do?"

"Does it matter right now, Jerry?"

"I guess not." He paced. "Shit. What the hell am I going to tell my captain?"

"Are you going to arrest us?"

"No, but I do have to bring you both in for questioning. I believe you, but I don't know what's going to happen to you or Vittorio. I'll do all I can to make sure you stay out of jail, but I can't promise anything. I'm going to have to call in more manpower."

"Can we try to get some rest until your backup gets here?"

"Why not?" Jerry waved his hand as if to dismiss me and pulled his cell phone out of his pocket.

I made a phone call of my own while Jerry was busy. "Courtney, I need you to meet me at the police station." I gave her the address. "I should be there in about an hour. I'll be busy for a while once I get there, but just wait for me, okay? There's no place safer for you to be." I didn't want her to be alone at the hotel.

I'd fallen asleep, and was woken by the sound of police sirens some time later. Vittorio and I were handcuffed and put in the back of separate police cars and driven to the station. It was unsettling to be on this side of the law, but I was too tired to think about it very hard.

At the police station, I had to repeat my story on the record. Steve Ericson, a cop I didn't know, conducted the interview while Jerry waited outside the interrogation room. It took even longer this time, as he was less inclined to believe me than Jerry. When I got to the part about my scars, I again asked for a knife.

"No way," Steven said.

A knock sounded on the door. Officer Ericson opened it, and Jerry came in. "Let her do it."

"No way," he said again. "I don't trust this wacko with a knife."

"Steve, she's telling the truth. I saw this myself. I'll stand by just in case, but give her a chance."

Steve made no move to do as Jerry told him, so Jerry gave me his knife again.

"You're crazy, man!" Steve backed as far away from me as possible, never taking his eyes off me.

Again, I cut my arm and called my power to heal it. Steve's eyes went wide as he tried to back even further away, into the wall if he could. "Alright, fine. I believe you; just knock that shit off."

I had already called my power back to me.

"I need a coffee break, Jerry," Steve said.

"Can I have some too?" I remembered how awful the coffee at the city station was, but anything was better than nothing.

The officers left, locking the door behind them. I may not be a suspect yet, but Steve wasn't going to take any chances with me. I wondered how well Jerry knew him.

About fifteen minutes later, Steve returned with two cups of coffee, looking calmer than when he left. He finished the interview an hour later, and told me to wait there, again locking the door behind him. As if I could go anywhere. I was so weak I could barely sit upright.

Jerry returned a while later. "They finished questioning Vittorio, and have decided to let you both go."

"Can I see him?"

Vittorio walked through the door. I ran to him and held him tight. It had only been a few hours since I last saw him, but I was still tired, my energy still depleted, and my power seemed to need Vittorio even more at times like these. "It's okay; they believe us," I whispered into his ear, inhaling the scent of his skin.

"Who's the girl waiting in the lobby for you?" Jerry asked.

"Just a friend. I figured we'd need a ride home." I was glad to hear Courtney was safe.

"Is she involved in any of this?"

"She doesn't know a thing about it." That much was true, at least for the moment. I wasn't sure how much we were going to tell her.

"Alright, but you better not be hiding anything from me. I'll call you when we need more information from you. And be careful," Jerry said.

We decided it would be safe to go back to Vittorio's since everyone except Neal was out of the picture for the time being.

CHAPTER FIFTY-NINE

It was late when we got back to Vittorio's. Vittorio went to make up the guest room, though I knew it was in perfect order, while I led Courtney to the kitchen.

"Do you want anything to eat or drink?" I asked.

"Just some water would be great. Thanks for letting me stay here."

I pulled out a chair for her.

"Can I ask you a question?"

"Anything." As I answered, I found I truly meant that. I liked the girl, and would truthfully answer anything she asked. I set a glass of water down on the table for her and filled a kettle to make tea for myself.

"Do you live here, too?"

"That's an easy one," I laughed, setting the kettle on the stove. "Kind of. I have my own place, and it's really just in the past few days Vittorio and I talked about me moving in here. I don't know if I'll get rid of my place, but I probably will. We've had a lot going on lately."

"You are so lucky. He's gorgeous!" she gushed and giggled.

I couldn't help but smile. "Luckier than I deserve to be, that's for sure. Come on, don't you have any harder questions than that?" I teased. I didn't know the girl well enough to know how to put her at ease, and I hoped light-hearted teasing would work.

"How did you meet Vittorio? And how on earth did you snag him? From what I've heard, he never dated anyone seriously until he met you."

"Gossip gets around, huh?"

Courtney blushed and looked down.

"It's okay; don't be embarrassed. I met him at The Chapel. I was sitting at the bar minding my own business, when Bryn - the bartender - gave me a drink I hadn't ordered, saying it was from Vittorio. I marched right up to thank him and introduce myself, and found myself rooted in place, staring like a damn fool. I have never been so awestruck by a man before; it was humiliating." The kettle screeched its readiness. "I couldn't fathom why he would be so interested in me, but I found out a few days later." I paused my story while I fixed my tea. I sat at the table with the mug of steaming Earl Grey tea, comforted by the aroma.

"Why was that?"

"Like you, I had no idea I had any power. Turns out my power is quite attracted to Vittorio's, and it made itself known to me in a rather embarrassing way."

Courtney gave me a questioning look. She wasn't going to make this easy on me.

"One night at The Chapel, he kissed me. Just a kiss, nothing major. It barely would have earned a PG rating, aside from the way it affected me."

"How is that?"

"My whole body felt like rubber. I almost fell, and when he caught me, it made the effect even stronger." My cheeks burned. "I wanted him more than I have ever wanted anyone before. He realized then I had power, and brought me here to try to explain it to me. I agreed to let him teach me to control it. When he tried to leave the guest room to let me sleep, my power protested. Had it not been for Samuel, well," I stared into my mug, letting my hair fall around my face, flustered at the prospect of telling Courtney. "I'm not sure even the dirtiest porn director would have wanted to film what I would have done to Vittorio."

When I finally looked back at Courtney, she was staring at me with her mouth open. "You're kidding?"

"I wish I was. He couldn't train me. Until I could control my power, I couldn't even be in the same room with him. Samuel had to train me, then he had to train us together until we could fully control our power together."

"You can control your power now, right?" She took a drink of water.

"Yes, mostly, but it still takes great concentration when I'm around Vittorio." I blushed again. "If I'm overly tired, I tend to lose a bit of control. Nothing like that first night, though." I left out the incident where I nearly jumped Vittorio's bones at The Chapel. If Courtney stuck around, I was sure she'd hear about it one way or another.

"What else can you do? What can I do?" Courtney leaned forward slightly.

"I can make people feel like they are being shocked by electricity. That's my method of combat, it seems. I can also heal people." I didn't tell her about the ability to bring people back from the dead. I wasn't ready for that to be common knowledge yet. Maybe never. It was way too Jesus Christy for me. "As for what you can do, time will tell. It seems almost everyone can do little tricks like the ball of light thing, but as for your more major abilities, we know you can see through glamour. You may or may not have others. Everyone is different."

"When will I know?" She was eager to learn.

"I don't know. Vittorio can answer questions like that better than I can. I'm still learning, too."

"But you're so strong."

It was my turn to give a questioning look.

"Everyone in the coven talks about you. They're either in awe of you or terrified of you."

I gaped at her in disbelief.

"It's true." She paused. "Are you really going to be the new Sacerdotessa?"

"I don't know. It's possible. I still have a lot to learn. But let me ask you something. How do you know so much about the coven?"

"Miriam tells me about it. She knows I want to join, and she thinks if I know more about it, Clavius will be more likely to accept me." She looked down into her lap. "Well, he would have been."

"Why do you want to join so badly?"

"At first, it was to piss off my mom. But the more I hung around The Chapel, the more I got to like the people there."

"You know this isn't a game? It's a religion. It's not something you should do just because you hate your mom."

"I know. I've been interested in witchcraft for a long time. I just never knew anyone for real until I met Miriam and her friends. And even then, I didn't know magic was real...or that I had any power." Courtney ran her finger around the rim of her glass, brow furrowed.

You can come save me anytime, love, I thought to Vittorio.

As soon as I did, he walked into the kitchen. "The guest room is ready if you would like to get some sleep."

"Can I ask you some questions first?" Courtney's expression was already under control.

"Of course." Vittorio sat at the table.

I went to make him a cup of tea, and refill mine.

"How do I learn how to use this power? And what else can I do?" Courtney asked.

"I will find someone in the coven to teach you. And there is no way to know that upfront. New abilities may manifest in time."

"What do you mean 'may?' "

"You may have other abilities, or you may not."

"But how can I protect myself?" Courtney had so much to learn. It was hard to believe I knew as little as she just a month ago.

"Not everyone has a combative power," Vittorio said.

"Do you?"

"Yes." Vittorio did not elaborate.

I realized I didn't know his combative power, either. Odd,

since we had already been through so much. I guess I hadn't been around for most of it, though, and things were chaotic the other night.

Again, Courtney did not push. She was very perceptive. It didn't take magic to read a person's body language if you knew what to look for.

"I think I'll go to bed now. Thanks for letting me stay here," she said.

"You are most welcome. You can stay as long as you like if you will feel safer here," I said as I led her to the guest room.

"I think Courtney has been through something rough," I said, finally in Vittorio's bedroom.

"Why do you say that, mio amore?"

"She's good at keeping her facial expressions in check. And she's very perceptive. She knows when to ask questions, and when not to push a point. Do you think she might be able to read people's minds or emotions?"

"I do not think she can read minds. That is a rare ability indeed, and is hard for the person possessing it to be unaware of. She shows no signs of it. It is possible she is an empath, however. Time will tell."

I waited for him to say more.

"Are you going to ask me?" He raised his eyebrow.

"Ask you what?" I didn't want to push him, either.

"How I protect myself."

"Oh, that." I tried to be nonchalant, but wanted desperately to know.

"Mio amore, do not play coy. I know you are curious." He smiled at me, and pulled me to him.

"I just figure if you want me to know, you'll tell me. I do find it interesting I haven't seen it yet considering what we've been through," I said, cuddling close.

"I have two combative skills. I am able to block power attacks, and turn their power back on them. I try to limit it to that."

"What's the other one?" I pulled away a little so I could look at him.

"I can drain one's life force."

"What do you mean?"

"Essentially, I can drain their energy and take it into myself. If I limit how much I drain, it will merely leave them weak. If I am not careful, it will kill them."

"That's how everyone's combative power works, isn't it? Too much and you kill your enemy?"

"Yes, but this is a little different. Bringing my enemy's energy into myself is usually unpleasant. Many think it would be a wonderful ability, because it makes me stronger. But it is someone else's life force, and it is often a negative force that I do not want in myself."

"Can't you drain them without taking their energy into yourself?"

"I have not figured out how, if it is possible. Imagine taking Neal's power. Neal is hateful, evil. That would leave a stain on your psyche. Once will not affect you strongly, but if you drain too many people, even a little, it will build up. I do not like the power. I would almost rather have no combative ability."

I shuddered at the thought. "I'm sorry."

"For what?"

"For asking. I can tell it causes you pain."

"Do not apologize. You deserve to know. It is the one aspect of myself which I have not been able to accept." He looked lost in a sad memory, but I did not push for details. I put my arms around him and kissed his cheek.

"You have the power to drain life, and I can give it back."

"I had not thought of it like that. An interesting observation, mio amore."

Interesting, indeed. I still wanted to know what all this meant, why he said I could do great things. "I'm scared of my power, Vittorio."

"It is nothing to be afraid of, mio amore."

"The power to bring people back to life, in particular. I mean, if word of that gets out, everyone and their dog will want me to bring their loved ones back to life. I can't do that."

"We will keep that a closely guarded secret. But I do not believe it works like that. I believe you have to have a close connection to the person, a strong desire for them to be alive."

"I hope you're right." I huddled close to him, as if he could make the Big Bad Monster go away. "Sometimes, I wish I could go back to being normal."

"I understand." He looked a little hurt.

"But then I remember it's all this craziness that brought me to you, and I wouldn't change a thing." That earned me a smile.

CHAPTER SIXTY

The next day, Vittorio gave me a quick rundown of the members of the coven, who was on our side, who was on Samuel's, and whom he was unsure of. There were far too many in the last two groups. We decided to go to The Chapel that night; delaying it would do no good. We both wanted more rest, but couldn't afford time to ourselves just yet. Vittorio also decided we both needed new outfits to wear for our reappearance at the club, something spectacular. He wanted to send me shopping with Sarah while he went on his own, but I refused to be separated from him. Partially because I was scared for myself, but mostly because I was scared for him. He agreed with no hesitation, sensing the prudence of staying together until this was all over.

Vittorio's new outfit was easier to pick out than mine. He opted for a cream white velvet tuxedo, shirt, vest, and tie. He did not let me see him in it when he tried it on. I teased him for acting like a girl. I knew what he was doing, though. I would spend the day impatient to see him in the beauty of his new clothes, anticipation rising, then would spend the evening impatient to see him out of them. I grinned at his manipulations.

He insisted I buy a white gown as well. "White isn't very Goth, is it?" I teased.

"We need to make a statement when we arrive. White will set us apart from everyone, and will signify the new beginning for us."

"And what new beginning is that?"

"Our new stance on the coven, against Clavius and his followers, and for justice and equality."

I tried on half a dozen gowns, but none felt right. When the shop girl brought the last one for me to try on, I caught my breath. I had seen that dress before. It was the dress I wore in the dream I had of marrying Vittorio the night I met him. It was perfect.

Sarah again helped me with my hair. She arranged it in a partial up-do, and curled the strands that trailed down my back. She also advised me to keep my makeup simple and earthy this time, to help me stand out from the rest of the crowd. My black and purple-streaked hair was a stunning contrast to the pale gown and makeup.

A knock at the door as I finished applying my lipstick demonstrated Vittorio's impeccable timing. Sarah went to let him in, leaving us alone. I turned from the mirror, excited to see him in his new tux. I caught my breath. Vittorio was always gorgeous, but tonight he affected me as strongly as he had when I first saw him. His thick, black hair fanned out in perfect contrast to his white tuxedo. He walked to me, gently pushed my jaw up, and kissed me. "Wow."

"Is the wow for the kiss, or my outfit?" he asked.

"Yes," I said, breathless.

He kissed me again.

"Wow," I said again.

Vittorio pulled a small, long box from the inner pocket of his jacket and handed it to me.

"What's this?" I asked, hesitant to accept what must surely be a very expensive piece of jewelry.

"Open it," he insisted, pushing the box into my hands.

I discovered a gorgeous diamond necklace that must have cost twice what I made in a year.

"Is this real?"

He nodded. Of course it was; Vittorio wouldn't give me cubic zirconia.

"Vittorio, I can't take this." I held it out to him.

"Why not?"

Why not, indeed? "It's too expensive."

"I do not think so. Nothing is too good for you." He took the necklace from the box and stood behind me to fasten it around my neck before I could protest further. He led me to the mirror, where I admired its beauty.

"Thank you."

"You are welcome, mio amore." He kissed the side of my neck, and I inhaled his scent. My pulse raced, and my power called to him. "Now, mio amore, you will mess up your perfect hair and makeup. Am I that tempting to you?"

"Do you even have to ask?"

He smiled and chuckled in response, the way only a man can when he knows how completely a woman desires him. "Let us go now. There will be plenty of time for that later." He held out his arm for me. "Shall we?"

I sighed in only partially mock disappointment. "If you insist. I love you, you know," I said, and kissed him gently on the lips, keeping my power firmly in check.

"Ti amo, troppo."

CHAPTER SIXTY-ONE

When we walked into The Chapel, everyone turned to stare at us. We must have been quite a sight in a sea of black and dark colors. I wished I could have seen us from an outsider's view. The crowd parted to let us pass, and I almost felt as if we were walking up the aisle on our wedding day. Courtney had gone home to change and get more clothes to bring back to Vittorio's. We thought it would look odd if she arrived with us, since we hadn't been close to her previously, and decided it would be better to keep that semblance of distance, at least for the moment.

When we got to the top of the balcony stairs, everyone stopped their conversation and watched us. I thought I would suffocate from the tension in the air. Vittorio did not seem to notice it, and acted as if nothing was wrong.

Courtney and Miriam sat on a couch across the way. Courtney gave me a little wave, while Miriam glared at me.

We sat down, Vittorio's arm around my shoulders, and Felicia immediately come to take our drink order. I opted for water, too nervous to risk cranberry juice with a white dress, while Vittorio ordered scotch and water.

A man I had seen before, but never met, sat in the chair across from us. "How are you, my friend?" he asked Vittorio.

"I have been better, but as well as can be expected. Emmett, it is my pleasure to introduce you to Elena, the love of my life. Elena, this is my good friend Emmett."

Emmett was six feet tall and muscular, with short dark hair and honey brown eyes. He looked to be in his late twenties, but wore

233

an old-fashioned suit straight from a Jimmy Stewart movie. He completed his look with a fedora and Chuck Taylor high tops.

I held out my hand to shake Emmett's, but he turned mine over and kissed the back of my hand. It was just a touch of lips through the glove, nothing as enticing as Vittorio's touch of lips to my skin. "Enchantee." He grinned boyishly.

I smiled. Something told me I could trust Emmett. "The shoes don't quite match the ensemble, Emmett," I said.

"True, but they're comfortable, and I hate dress shoes," he said.

"What news do you have for us, Emmett?" Vittorio asked.

"Everyone is restless. With both Clavius and Aerin dead, and Elizabeth in the hospital, you are the only person in the chain of power left. Of course your allies are happy, but your enemies are plotting ways to be rid of you."

"Do you know of any of these plots?"

"There is nothing solid. Now that Samuel and Jonah are in jail, and Neal is missing, no one has quite enough initiative to take control."

"Neal is missing?" Vittorio raised his eyebrows.

"No one seems to know where he is, and if they do, they are holding the secret very tightly."

"Interesting. I wonder if he has deserted Samuel's cause. He always struck me as weak and indecisive. Maybe he is laying low until this is all over, waiting to side with whoever is victorious."

"Will you be our new Sacerdote, and Elena our Sacerdotessa?" No beating around the bush for this guy.

"It is too soon to tell. If it means keeping Samuel out of the picture, yes, I will, but Elena has much to learn before she can make a decision such as that. She is not even familiar with our ways yet."

"I will," I said.

Vittorio stared at me. "Mio amore?"

"If you desire it, and the coven accepts it, I will be

Sacerdotessa." A knot I hadn't known was there loosened in my stomach.

"How can you be sure?"

"What happened between us last night…I'm not sure how to explain it, but I know this is the right decision, that it's what I'm meant to do."

Vittorio smiled and embraced me.

"We will fight Samuel's followers?" Emmett asked.

"Unfortunately, I do not think we have any other choice. I neither want to fight them nor leave the coven in their hands. I care for our family far too much to leave them to that fate. I hope to make this as painless as possible for everyone, in every manner."

Courtney walked over and interrupted our conversation. "Hey," she said, standing awkwardly.

"Why don't you sit down?" I asked, motioning to the empty seat next to Emmett.

He introduced himself to Courtney the same way he had to me.

She giggled and looked down to her lap, then looked back at him and smiled.

"Can I ask you something, Courtney?" There was still something that seemed too coincidental.

"Sure, what?"

"How did you meet Miriam?" I asked.

"It was kind of strange. I met her in my art class, but she talked to me first. It seemed odd. I mean, I didn't exactly fit in with her style…I'm sure my mom gave you an old picture of me."

I nodded.

"She seemed really nice, though, and I liked her style. I'd been having a hard time making friends in college so I didn't question it."

"And Elizabeth is Miriam's aunt, right?"

"Yeah, but what does that matter?" Courtney thought for a moment. "Oh my god, you think they set me up from the beginning?"

"I don't know, but it does seem like a big coincidence."

Courtney stood and looked about to storm back over to Miriam. "I'm going to give her a piece of my mind."

I grabbed her hand. "Courtney, wait. I wouldn't say anything just yet. If I'm right, it could be dangerous. I'd wait till everything blows over before you confront her."

She sat back down, slumping. "I guess you're right. So, I'm supposed to pretend like nothing happened and we're still friends?" She sighed. "Alright, I'll try."

"Courtney, Emmett has the power of glamour. Would you mind if we tried something to test if you are really able to see through it?" Vittorio asked.

"I guess not," she said, fidgeting with the hem of her skirt. "I'm still trying to get used to the idea of magic being real is all."

"Elena, do you have something in your purse we can use, something Courtney has not seen before?" Emmett asked.

I turned to hide my purse from Courtney and pulled out a small, red hairbrush. Emmett made it appear to be silver, and then I held it up for Courtney to see. "What color is my brush?"

"Red," she said, as if it was the stupidest question ever.

"Vittorio, what color do you see?" Emmett asked.

"Silver. Emmett, please drop the glamour on the brush." It appeared red again. "Now what color do you see Courtney?"

"Still red. But this can't be real."

"It is real."

Emmett reached for Courtney's hand and she took his gratefully.

The hair on my arms stood on end, and the temperature in the room dropped. I knew it was not the physical temperature, though. A new power was in the room. I knew that power. Neal had come out of hiding.

CHAPTER SIXTY-TWO

"You should go back to Miriam so she doesn't think anything is wrong," Emmett tactfully turned Courtney away from the danger we might be in. Neal approached us as she walked away.

"Vittorio. Elena. You look well." He sounded disappointed. "I did not expect to see you here tonight. In fact, I did not expect to ever see you again." He made no secret of the plans Samuel evidently had for us.

"Sorry to disappoint you," I said.

"I heard you have discovered a new power in yourself."

"Oh?" I said, not wanting to give anything away. The only new power was having brought Vittorio back to life, and I wasn't sure I could repeat that performance. Even so, how would he know about that?

"I have my ways," he said, revealing a new power of his own - mind reading. "And if you can do it once, you can certainly do it again, given enough incentive." He held a knife to Vittorio's neck.

How had he made it there so fast without any of us seeing the movement?

"Dear Elena, you know everyone has different powers. Did you not think speed could be one of them? Now, let's see. It would be a shame to get blood on this beautiful, white tux, don't you think, Vittorio? How can we avoid that?" Neal looked upwards, pretending to think. I knew he already had a plan, though, and tried to come up with my own quickly. I would have to act upon it quickly, as well, before Neal read it in my thoughts. "I know, you can banish Elena from the city, swear your loyalty to Samuel, and

237

give up your position as La Guardia."

"Do you really think I would agree to that?"

"No, but it was worth a try. Perhaps I can banish both of you. No, you're both too stubborn, that would never work. A pity. I guess I'll just have to kill you, then torture Elena until she sides with us. Her power would be very useful." Neal pushed the knife harder against Vittorio's neck, not yet drawing blood. Would he really kill him here? I didn't think so, and was happy for the time that bought us. Unless, that is, he proved to be that crazy. Insanity glinted in Neal's eyes, but it was the type accompanied by cold precision and caution rather than recklessness. He pushed upwards with the knife. "Let's go. You will walk out in front of me, but I will have this knife ready for any false move you make."

Vittorio stood. I followed, not sure if it was what Neal wanted, but not wanting to let Vittorio out of my sight. When Neal didn't argue, I assumed it was the right decision. Emmett started to follow, as well.

"Not you. Sit."

Emmett sat.

"On second thought, I don't want you calling for help after we leave. Not that you know where we're going. But better to be safe. Yes, come with us." Did he really believe Emmett was the only one here who would call for help?

"Yes, because no one else can see what's going on. I have clouded their minds. Emmett has the power to resist me, though." He laughed when he looked at my face. "You look so shocked, Elena. Did you not believe I was this powerful? Samuel has an idea of my power, but only Clavius knew how powerful I truly am. I like it that way. At times like this, I am able to take people by surprise. And their shock is so amusing. The secret strength of my power is why Clavius left me behind, in case anything went wrong while he was away. Now go."

We filed down the stairs and out the front door of The Chapel. I wanted to look at Bryn, but was afraid to give anything away, afraid to put her in danger. I wondered if Emmett had power other than the ability to resist mind manipulation. I couldn't very well ask him in front of Neal, but it would have been helpful to know.

Emmett is weak. That is his only power. We will think of something. Neal is very fast, so we must be extremely careful.

Since he can read minds, can he read what we're saying to each other now?

Most likely. We must be careful. I no longer heard Vittorio in my mind.

"Get in the car." Neal unlocked a dark blue Suburban with windows so darkly tinted one couldn't see through them. He showed no sign of having read our silent conversation. We got in the back of the Suburban and Neal started driving. I huddled against Vittorio, scared of what might happen to him if we didn't find a way out of this. The thought of what Neal would do to me never crossed my mind; I didn't care about that.

Neal stopped in a deserted area of a rundown part of town. "Get out, and stand by the car." The three of us obeyed, still having no plan. "Not you, Elena. Stay in the car."

I didn't move.

"Do it!" he said, drawing his knife.

I got into the passenger side front seat, away from where Vittorio and Emmett stood, so I could open the door quickly if I had to.

"Samuel thought you would be a problem, Vittorio, but he never foresaw just how much of one. Your little plaything doesn't help matters. But she seems to have some useful powers, so we'll keep her around. Watching me kill you might convince her to cooperate with me to save her own life."

"No! Don't hurt him! I'll do whatever you want, just don't hurt him!" I screamed from inside the Suburban.

"Such strong love. Whatever I want. You have no idea what you are promising."

"I don't care." Tears streamed down my face.

"Do you see, Vittorio? She cries for you. She is strong, but when it comes to you, she is weaker than anyone I have ever met. Would she betray you so easily, just to save your life?"

"She would never betray me." Even through the window, the conviction in Vittorio's words rang clear. It warmed my heart that he could believe that so strongly, even after what I had done.

"That's not what she is saying, though. Are you so blind?"

"You can read her thoughts. Why don't you see for yourself?" What was Vittorio doing? Why would he tell Neal to invade my mind?

I watched Neal cock his head as he concentrated. Had I not known what he was doing, I would never have been wiser. He left no trace, no whisper or touch in my mind as he read it. He was dangerous, this I knew.

"You are right. She believes she would never betray you, yet still she says she would do anything to save your life. Interesting. I do not see how she can believe both so strongly. But that doesn't matter. Killing you will cause her great pain, which I will enjoy immensely."

I caught the slightest movement, like a flicker of light, and knew Neal was making his move to murder the man I loved. I was powerless to stop him.

CHAPTER SIXTY-THREE

"No!" I screamed. I wished for Vittorio to be alright, wished for Neal to be the one to die. As I wished that with all my being, time seemed to nearly stop. I saw Neal running toward Vittorio, the knife aimed for his heart. I saw him trip, though there was nothing in the way of his foot. He fell, arms flailing. I threw open the door and ran to Vittorio. It seemed to take ages, even though he was only a few feet from me. I watched as his arms reached for me. I didn't understand what was happening. Was I in shock?

Neal landed and his knife plunged into his own heart. Time resumed its normal pacing. I stared at Neal in horror. "Oh my god, I killed him!"

"Of course you didn't, mio amore." Vittorio knelt next to me on the ground, holding me to him, trying to comfort me. I hadn't realized I had collapsed to my knees next to Neal's body.

"I did. I killed him," I sobbed.

"Why do you say that?" Vittorio gently turned me to look at him.

"I saw him coming at you with the knife, and I wished for him to die instead of you."

"He was moving too fast; you couldn't have seen him."

"But I did, and I wished for you to be okay, and for him to die. Then," I could barely talk through my sobs.

"Calm down, mio amore. Then what?" He stroked my hair, trying to calm me.

"Everything slowed down, like slow motion in a movie. Neal tripped, but there was nothing in his way, and now he's dead and it's my fault. I don't want to be a murderer!" I cried hysterically. This couldn't be happening. It had to be a dream. I hadn't just killed Neal with my thoughts. I always knew there was a possibility I would have to shoot someone on the job; some of my investigations were dangerous, and that's why I carried a gun. But that would be self-defense. This, I had plainly wished for Neal to die. I didn't want this. I wanted Vittorio safe, yes, but not at the cost of someone else's life. Not when it was clearly my fault that someone was dead.

"You can change this, mio amore," Vittorio said, holding me.

"How? I can't go back in time."

"But you can bring Neal back to life."

"I don't know how." My stomach clenched; I was going to be sick.

"You did it before. I believe if you simply wish strongly enough for him to be alive, you will succeed. Put your hands on him, hold him if you must, wish for him to live, but you must truly want it with all your being."

"I do want him to be alive." If he were alive, it would mean I wasn't a murderer, indirectly or otherwise.

"Then make it so."

"But what if I fail?"

He held my face in his hands and looked me in the eyes. "You have to try. Won't you feel a little better knowing you tried and failed, than if you didn't try at all?"

I nodded.

"Take him in your arms. Picture him alive, his heart beating. Picture him free of blood and whole. I know you can do this, mio amore."

The confidence I saw in his face scared me. He believed in me so completely. No one had believed in me like that since I told my mom I was trying out for the lead part in the musical my freshman year.

I moved closer to Neal, then rolled him onto his back and lay my hands on his chest. I did not want to hold him if I didn't have to. I pictured him alive as Vittorio said, and called upon my power to bring him back, to heal him and make his heart beat again. I wished for him to be alive, wrapped him in healing energy. I tried to believe I could do this. I pushed everything out of my mind other than thoughts of healing Neal.

After a few minutes, Neal twitched. His heart beat softly, chest rising with breath. I did it! He was alive!

Vittorio had the presence of mind to make sure the knife was not within Neal's reach. I was about to stand when he opened his eyes and looked at me. Fear clenched my gut. What would he do? Did he have strength to harm me? Did he know it was my fault he was almost dead?

"You." That one word seemed to take much effort. "How?"

I shook my head back and forth. I didn't know. How could I explain it to Neal? Even if I had known, I wouldn't have told him. He could read my mind. Let him figure it out on his own.

"But I'm alive. I don't understand. Why would you do that?"

"I didn't want responsibility for your death." I slumped against Vittorio.

"You are weaker than I thought. I could be of no concern to you now, and no one would know how, yet still you saved me. I don't understand."

"You are too evil to understand," I said.

Neal looked for his knife.

"You won't be needing this anymore," Vittorio said, holding the knife.

Neal tried to stand, and stumbled. Emmett helped Neal into the third row of the Suburban, fishing the keys from his pocket when he passed out. "What now?" Emmett asked.

"Guess we should call Jerry. He's going to love this," I said.

CHAPTER SIXTY-FOUR

When Jerry arrived, he handcuffed Neal and put him in the back of his car. I told him everything that had happened. Jerry's backup took us all to the station to give our reports.

"Jerry, can I ask you something unrelated to this?" I asked when I was finished.

"What?"

"Are we ever going to be able to be friends again?" I was pretty certain the answer would be no.

He thought for a while. "I don't know."

"Thank you for being honest about that." It was better than I expected.

"I'm having a hard time with all this magic mumbo jumbo." He crossed his arms.

"I hope we will. You mean a lot to me. But this is part of who I am now. I'm still basically the same person I always was, there's just more to me now."

"I know, but it's going to take some time for me to come to terms with it. This isn't exactly normal stuff, you know. Magic isn't supposed to be real."

"Who says what's supposed to be real and not? Just because we don't understand something doesn't mean it doesn't exist. You can't just wish it away." If that were the case, I'd wish Kevin back to being alive.

"I know. What's all this about the coven?"

"If Vittorio and I manage to stay alive, chances are we'll be named Sacerdote and Sacerdotessa of the coven - High Priest and

Priestess," I corrected myself, realized Jerry didn't know the Italian words. "Now that Clavius is dead, and his wife Aerin, the Sacerdotessa, was killed six months ago in a burglary, they need someone to step up. Samuel wants the position for himself. Neal probably does, too. They wouldn't be good for it, though."

"And you would? You don't even know anything about witchcraft." He paused. "Do you?"

"I have a lot to learn, it's true, but I'd be better than anyone they would have in my place. They would have had Elizabeth before -" I stared at my hands, picking the skin around my nails, trying to force back tears.

"Why are you doing this?" The sudden softness to Jerry's tone made me look at him.

"It's hard to explain." I went back to picking my nails.

"Humor me and try."

"I know it's the right thing to do. I know it's why I'm here, that I'm meant to be Sacerdotessa. Even though I don't know much about it all, I know it's my purpose."

"But how do you know?" Jerry stood and paced.

"You wouldn't believe me." I didn't want to tell Jerry, but did want to mend our friendship if that was at all possible.

"Tell me anyway." He stopped and looked me in the eye, standing very still.

"The goddess told me." I sat very still.

"You're right, I don't believe you," he said, turning away from me, shoulders slumping.

"Why not?" I yelled, pushing myself up from the chair and knocking it to the floor in the process. "Christians get messages from their God all the time. Why can't pagans get messages from goddess? It's the same thing."

He spun around, fists clenched. "Christians aren't going to burn in hell when they die."

"Is that so? Charles Manson was Christian, wasn't he? Hitler was a Christian. Do you think they're going to heaven? And anyway, I don't believe in heaven or hell, so I don't really care about that. I'm just trying to live the best life I can and stay out of everyone else's way. Everyone else is making that pretty damned difficult."

"I'm sorry, Elena."

I didn't know what he was apologizing for; there was so much. "Maybe we should stick to business until you come to terms with this. I don't know how much more of your hurtful words I can take."

"I said I'm sorry." He looked at the floor.

"Can I go now?"

Jerry nodded, and I walked out without another word.

CHAPTER SIXTY-FIVE

The next day was Kevin's funeral. His parents glared at me the moment I walked into the church. I hadn't had time to talk to them, so I went to offer my condolences. They walked away when they saw me headed toward them, making an already difficult situation even harder.

Vittorio put his arm around my waist and led me to a pew to sit down. Hot tears streamed down my face as soon as the service began. I was glad I hadn't bothered with makeup. He tried to soothe me with his power, but there was no comforting me that day, no matter how strong he might be.

I almost lost it entirely when I walked past the casket for the final viewing. I knelt by the coffin, grasping Kevin's hand, sobbing, "I'm sorry," over and over again. Had I been any more hysterical, Vittorio probably would have carried me out. As it was, he simply put his arm around me and supported all my weight. I opted to skip the cemetery, for which I'm certain Kevin's parents were grateful.

Vittorio ran a hot bath when we got home and held me. My exhaustion finally let his power do its job and soothe me, enough for me to fall asleep, anyway.

I woke sometime in the middle of the night from a nightmare. Kevin was in his casket. His eyes opened, and he stared right at me. "Why didn't you save me?" he asked.

"I didn't know I could. You know I would have had I known," I cried.

"You knew. You saved Vittorio, but not me." Only his lips

247

moved.

"I didn't know how, I swear. Kevin, I'm so sorry, please don't be angry." I don't know where I was in the dream; floating above his casket, maybe.

"It's your fault I'm dead." Cold, dead eyes stared at me.

I woke screaming, and only stopped when Vittorio put his arms around me. "What is wrong, mio amore?"

"Nightmare." When I calmed a little, I told him.

"It is merely your subconscious feeling guilty. I am positive Kevin does not blame you for his death."

"How can you know that?"

"Kevin did not strike me as the blaming type, especially with his best friend. You must not blame yourself."

"That's easy for you to say," I sulked as he held me.

"I understand, mio amore. If there is anything I can do to help, you know I will do it." He stroked my hair.

"Just hold me while I try to go back to sleep. Though I'm not sure that's possible."

Turns out it was. I fell asleep almost immediately. Hooray for exhaustion.

EPILOGUE

A month later, I was initiated into the coven. There is still no Sacerdote or Sacerdotessa, but everyone knows it will be Vittorio and me. I just need more time to learn the ways of witchcraft before I can step up.

Courtney does not stay with us anymore. She moved in with Emmett, and is learning to control her power nicely, although no other abilities have manifested for her. Thankfully, she's no longer friends with Miriam.

I finally moved out of my half of the duplex into Vittorio's house. I helped Kevin's parents clean out his half at the same time. It was difficult to say the least. They still don't understand what happened, and blame me for their son's death. They never liked me much anyway, and since I do feel responsible, I don't fault them. I fully accept the blame, even though Vittorio tries to convince me not to.

I visit Kevin's grave at least once a week to talk to him. He never answers, but it's soothing to think he might be listening to me. I still have nightmares, but they are growing less frequent than they were in the first week after his death. I don't think it helped that I had missed a month's worth of therapy sessions. I am finally back on a weekly schedule, and have even more crap to work through now.

Samuel's father, CEO of Porter Industries, accelerated the plans he had for retirement after the embarrassment his son caused. He offered the position to Vittorio, who, after much consideration, accepted.

Elizabeth will likely be in the mental hospital the rest of her life. Samuel, Jonah, and Neal have their trials scheduled. I can't wait for them to be over, for us to be safe again.

Hints of our power leaked to the media, and there is a lot of speculation about it. I am not looking forward to when the truth comes out publicly during the trial. The world is going to change.

THANK YOU

Thank you so much for taking the time to read *Divided*. I know your time is valuable, but if you can take a few minutes to leave a review on Amazon I would appreciate that so much. Leaving a review is one of the best things you can do to help me out, aside from telling your friends and family about my work.

Look for the exciting sequel, *Ravaged*, due out in late 2013. Exact date to be announced, but you can stay informed at my website, www.JenniferSights.com, where you can also sign up for my email list. I promise never to spam you.